The
GENTLE
WARRIOR

A CARIBBEAN JOURNEY
OF TRAGEDY AND TRIUMPH

SKIP JOHNSON

The
GENTLE
WARRIOR

A CARIBBEAN JOURNEY
OF TRAGEDY AND TRIUMPH

SKIP JOHNSON

Cover and Interior Design by Dino Marino | dinomarinodesign.com

Copy Editing by Jessica Andersen | jessicalandersen.com

Proofreading by Linda Dutro l lindadutro@gmail.com

Paperback ISBN: 979-8-9871654-8-5

eBook ISBN: 979-8-9871654-7-8

"Our chief want is someone who
will inspire us to be
what we know we could be."

—Ralph Waldo Emerson

ACKNOWLEDGMENTS

Thank you as always to my extraordinary team that helped bring yet another project together: Editor Jessica Andersen, Proofreader Linda Dutro, Cover Designer and Interior Format Specialist Dino Marino, and Web Designer Emily Grimaldi.

Additionally, I'm grateful once again to my Advance Review Team. A launch is the critical foundation of a book's success, and your work helps ensure that each book I write gets off to a great start. Thank you!

OTHER BOOKS BY SKIP JOHNSON

All books available at www.skipjohnsonauthor.com

The Mystic's Gift:
A Story About Loss, Letting Go . . .
and Learning to Soar

(Book 1 in The Mystic's Gift/Royce Holloway series)

A spellbinding, deeply moving story that is quickly becoming a self-help classic. Following a sudden, unimaginable personal tragedy at a point in his midlife when Royce Holloway thought he had it all, he is introduced to a wise, exotic, enchanting mentor named Maya, who takes Royce on a powerful journey of courageous self-discovery and incredible possibilities.

What he learns on this captivating, often poignant trek across two continents will change him in a powerful way, but you may find that the life changed most . . . is yours.

The Gentleman's Journey:
A Heartwarming Story of Courage,
Compassion, and Wisdom

(Book 2 in The Mystic's Gift/Royce Holloway series)

Five years after that glorious week when Maya shared six life-changing principles from an ancient secret book of wisdom with him, Royce is ready for a new chapter—to push his skills and his life to a higher level and make an even greater impact on the world.

In fact, he feels something is *leading* him to do that very thing . . .

So much so, that when Royce's journey takes him to the spectacular, historical Jekyll Island Club Hotel on the Georgia coast, it doesn't surprise him one bit when he "coincidentally" meets a mysterious, well-seasoned world traveler, a traveler whose life was *destined* to intersect with Royce Holloway's—in an unforgettable way for them both.

Join Royce on this powerful, spellbinding trek full of mystics, miracles, and inspirational stories.

You may find *your* life will never be the same again . . .

The Treasure in Antigua

(Book 3 in The Mystic's Gift/Royce Holloway series)

When Royce Holloway ends up on the magnificent island of Antigua, it's far from a Caribbean vacation. Instead, he finds himself on an incredible journey to locate a sacred, priceless treasure—one that Godfrey Tillman said would deeply impact Royce—and deeply impact the world.

If the carefully hidden prize could ever be found . . .

Along the way, Royce is led through a series of "coincidental" meetings with wise, inspirational mentors from all walks of life, who somehow seem part of a mysterious, bigger plan to guide him in reaching his destination.

Join Royce on his captivating, empowering, and often poignant trek across beautiful Antigua, and as you meet the different teachers on his path, you'll likely find the "student" whose life is changed most . . . is you.

The Lottery Winner's Greatest Ride: A Millionaire, a Young Reporter . . . and a Journey to Find What Matters Most

When Phillip Westford won the biggest lottery in history, he never dreamed there would be a price to pay.

A very *large* price that would shake his world to the core . . .

But just when he is at his breaking point, Phillip meets a mysterious old Irishman named Patrick O'Rourke who claims he knows the secret for getting the distraught young man back to happiness.

That is, *if* Phillip is willing to undertake a trek to find three wise mentors across the globe.

Join Phillip on a magnificent train ride as he shares the inspiring, incredible story of his journey of transformation with Juliette McKelvey, a young journalist who is on her own desperate journey to rebuild her crumbling life.

It's a ride to happiness you'll soon realize . . . you were *destined* to be on.

The Statue's Secret:
The Answers We Seek Can Often Be Found
In The Most Unlikely Places

Prominent Newport lawyer David Langley is a tormented man consumed by anxiety, guilt, and regret as his world falls apart more and more each day.

Until . . .

He fortuitously comes across an ancient Caribbean statue, which is soon verified as one of the most magnificent, sacred artifacts ever unearthed.

A relic that had a unique blessing bestowed upon it for the benefit of its fourteenth-century owner—and for all future owners . . .

A blessing that it seems could finally lead David on a path to a transformed life.

That is, *if* David can find his way to a mystical meeting with three wise, carefully chosen mentors at a remote location deep within the Dominican Republic jungle . . . within 48 hours.

Otherwise, the statue and its remarkable gift will vanish forever.

As David frantically, desperately makes his way to his final Dominican destination and the opportunity for an inspired new life, you'll find yourself enthusiastically cheering him on every step of the way.

Then, at some point you may realize the one who is truly on the journey . . . is *you*.

The Cobbler of Cape Town: A Tale of Courage, Love, and Transformation

In the 1930s, years before South Africa's famous freedom movement began, a humble, wise cobbler named Eli was dreaming of happiness in Cape Town.

It was a bold dream about prosperity for everyone in his divided land—not just the privileged few.

At the same time, a distraught yet determined eighteen-year-old named Lucas arrived in Cape Town from Holland on what he hoped would be a transformative, healing journey of service after suffering a family tragedy.

When destiny brings the pair together, Eli and Lucas make a divinely inspired pact to lay the groundwork for empowerment and hope for the oppressed people.

With The Cobbler's Creed as their sacred compass, the men embark on the impossible task of bringing happiness and belief to Cape Town . . .

But the ruthless, separative South African government learns of their progress, and the politicians begin fearing the ever-growing influence of the two men, vowing to stop them at any cost.

With their lives in danger and time running out, Eli and Lucas find themselves facing adversity that tests every ounce of their strength and courage.

Set in the enchanting, awe-inspiring African landscape, The Cobbler of Cape Town is a gripping tale and an inspirational guide for those on a pilgrimage to overcome fear, doubt, and heartache—and make the world a better place.

The Innkeeper's Journal: A Tale of Self-Discovery

Set in a picturesque town on the Georgia coast, it's the story of a wealthy, entitled young couple from Boston, Nick and Maggie Reynolds, who are struggling through a relationship that seems headed for a bitter divorce.

Then, on a road trip to Florida, in a final, desperate attempt to rekindle their formerly fairy-tale marriage, they fortuitously take a detour that could change everything . . .

Stopping at a quaint bed and breakfast on the island of St. Simons, the pair meets the kind, jovial, yet mysterious coastal innkeeper Vince van Note.

It's Vince who soon introduces them to a powerful set of secretive, life-enhancing principles called The Four Truths, written in a journal by one of the most famous painters in history, over a hundred years ago.

When the innkeeper sends Maggie and Nick on daily "assignments" across the island to seek out magnificent manifestations of The Four Truths all around them, their eyes began opening to the unimaginable possibilities . . .

They start to understand how a life of greater peace, appreciation, joy, compassion, and love may have been available to them all along.

If they had only known The Four Truths . . .

Join Nick and Maggie as they take a life-changing journey through the spectacular Golden Isles of Georgia, frantically trying to recover true happiness and love for each other.

Hidden Jewels of Happiness:
Powerful Essays for Finding and Savoring
the Gifts on Your Journey

A book of wisdom, encouragement, and empowerment for dealing with life's daily challenges. Let Skip reveal to you the seemingly hidden gifts that are all around us, waiting to be discovered and savored. You'll feel inspired, enlightened, and happier with every page.

Grateful for Everything:
Learning, Living, and Loving
the Great Game of Life

A deeply engaging book that provides a blueprint for using the power of gratitude to increase your happiness and fulfillment. You'll find delightful stories and practical ideas for turning your life into a great game to play each day, instead of a dreary battle to be fought.

TABLE OF CONTENTS

CHAPTER 1

"Come on, Son, get a move on!"

Bethanie Pérez, the petite, thirty-year-old former Dominican Republic beauty queen grinned as the young boy rushed into the kitchen, smiling.

"I'm hurrying, Momma. I still can't believe we're going on this trip!"

The woman gave a half shrug and grinned again. "I told you someday you were going to see the world. In fact, I think I said you would someday *change* the world. Today we are going to let you see a little of what is out there besides Punta Grande."

The boy's golden face lit up. "I've thought about how you worked so hard to make this happen, Momma. I can't wait."

Bethanie leaned down toward her eleven-year-old son and placed her hands on each side of his head. "Liam, when your father died, I wanted to make sure you still had a wonderful life. I am happy to have had my job as a housekeeper for as long as I did—so few people here in the Dominican Republic even have jobs. Since the family I have worked for is moving away, I thought now would be perfect to take time just for us. Then I'll find a new job."

She smiled. "For the Molinas to send us on a cruise to thank me for all my years of service was an unexpected and welcome surprise."

The boy nodded and listened carefully as his mother continued.

"Your father was a noble man—a great man. As you know, he named you Liam, which means 'strong-willed warrior and protector,' because he knew you would have the same spirit as he did—and I can see it in you, too. Yes, you are a warrior—but also a *gentle* warrior."

Liam shook his head and rolled his eyes playfully. "I know, Momma, I know. You always say that." He hesitated and added, "Even though . . . the children at school who make fun of me don't see it that way. I just wish I wasn't 'the boy with no father.'"

Bethanie tilted her head, put her arms tenderly around him, and stroked his soft, jet-black hair. "I know it is painful, my son. But I have *also* told you many times that their words do not matter. There will always be people like that in your life—people who tease you because deep down, they want to be like you. You are the kindest, bravest young man I know."

The Dominican woman glanced at her watch and abruptly changed the subject. "We'll talk more about this when we are on the cruise ship. We should be going now. It's going to be an unforgettable trip!"

With that, the young boy turned back toward his room where he grabbed his neatly packed suitcase.

Bethanie's voice called after him, "Did you make your bed, Liam?"

"Yes, Momma, every day, just like you taught me."

She nodded as he entered the room again. "Alright then. Everything in the house is organized and ready for us to be gone . . ."

The boy pointed his finger spiritedly and cut in with a broad smile. "For a whole week, right?"

"Yes, yes, for a whole week. Now let's get going!" She stepped behind him, placed her hands on his shoulders, and guided him out the open door.

Walking down the stairs of the home's small front porch, she paused. Then glancing back wistfully, she whispered to herself, "I never thought we would be doing this without you, Ernesto, but I am grateful you helped us make it come true for Liam." Looking heavenward, she gently made the sign of the cross, hesitated again, then stepped quickly to the small white car where Liam was now waiting.

"How did you get down here so fast?" she wondered aloud with a laugh.

Liam shrugged and beamed. "Father always said I would make a great sprinter."

"Yes, that's true, he did say that." Her lips turned up into a broad smile.

After Liam helped his mother lift their black suitcases into the trunk, the pair climbed into the front seats, and Bethanie started the ignition.

"Drive fast, Momma. I can't wait to get there!"

She shook her head and her eyes crinkled. "You know we must obey the laws of the country. The last thing we want is to get a ticket as we are leaving for our trip. It's only an hour and a half to the port in Santo Domingo, so be patient, we'll get there."

Liam nodded as his mother guided the small car out smoothly onto the side street, headed toward the bay—and to the start of an incredible adventure that lay ahead.

CHAPTER 2

As they reached the main road, Bethanie squinted at the highway sign. "Ah, yes, sixty-five miles. This should be an easy trip." She added, "How about I tell you a story?"

Liam beamed. Even at eleven years old, there was nothing he enjoyed more than his mom's creative tales.

Bethanie thought for a moment. "There once was a little boy who was born on a beautiful, tropical island of paradise. His mother and father loved him dearly."

She paused, glanced over, and noted his sudden poignant countenance. "I miss him, Momma. Even after all these years, I miss him so much."

She nodded solemnly. "I know, my son. I do, too. But he is looking down on us and smiling, knowing that we have gone on living. It hasn't been easy, but no mother loves her son more than I love you—and I always will."

His lips turned up as he gently pointed at his mother. "And no son loves his mother more than I love you, Momma—and *I* always will."

She grinned appreciatively and continued her story. "When Liam Pérez was born, the world took notice.

God smiled and said, 'This young boy is something special. He will change the world—just watch.'"

"That's my favorite part of the story, every time." He rubbed his hands together, and a broad grin spread across his face.

"Yes," she added with a nod. "People came from far and wide to see him. 'Ah, look, this is Liam the Great,' they would say."

Liam smiled again, then balled his hands into fists and raised them mockingly into the sky. "Yes, Liam, the great—but gentle—warrior, right, Momma?"

She raised her eyebrows and nodded reassuringly. "Oh yes indeed."

"As he grew, people came from all around to meet this young man. They would say, 'Liam, we have heard you are going to change the world, and we believe it— you will do great things!'"

Liam leaned in toward his mother as she continued, "When Liam got older, he went to school and then to university, and he went on to become a very famous man, yet a man who was kind to all he met."

She winked. "But he never forgot his mother."

Liam leaned over and put his arms around the woman, hugging her with all his might. "Never, Momma, never would I do that."

Her eyes sparkled. "I'll tell more of the story later—this is our exit." She pointed ahead excitedly. "Look, there's our ship in the distance!"

Liam craned his neck and saw the large cruise vessel docked, ready for passengers to step aboard.

"Oh, Momma, I can't believe it! I never thought I would be getting on a ship—and now we will be on one for a whole week!"

Bethanie's lips turned up into a smile as she steered her compact car into the crowded lot. "Here we are," she added as she nestled the vehicle carefully into a tight spot.

"Only a few steps from the ship. How lucky is that?!"

Liam shook his head and said with a grin, "We are *blessed*, Momma."

"Yes, that we are, my son. That we are."

Bethanie stepped out of the car as Liam unbuckled his seatbelt and followed suit. They each closed their doors and walked to the back of the vehicle. Then Liam raised the trunk lid and began to reach for the luggage.

"I'll get those, Son."

Liam shook his head. "Momma, remember, I'm Liam the Great. I'm strong!" He reached past his mother's outstretched arms, grabbed the first suitcase, and set it on the ground next to his mother. He then reached in and carefully pulled out the other.

Turning to her, he smiled broadly.

"Yes," she affirmed as she reached her hand out and rubbed Liam's head lovingly. "You are for sure a strong young man."

The pair rolled their suitcases behind them toward the waiting ship. As they approached, a tall, thin, dark-skinned man announced loudly, "All aboard! Ship leaves in thirty minutes. May I have your tickets, please?"

Bethanie reached into her beige purse and withdrew two folded papers. "Here you go, Sir." She flashed a smile at Liam as the man took the forms, opened them, and looked them over.

"Mrs. Pérez?" he asked, squinting over his reading glasses.

She nodded.

He turned to Liam. "I assume you are *Mr.* Pérez?"

Liam grinned and nodded.

"I'll take those suitcases for you, and you can follow the ramp up to the main deck. Your room will be at the end of the ship, on the right—number 7."

Bethanie turned to Liam, then took a deep breath. "Are you ready?"

He bobbed his head and then grabbed his mother's hand as they walked up the gangway, slowly and steadily, taking in the smell and moist feel of the sea breeze and the sound of the seagulls squawking.

Finally, they reached the top, and Liam pointed toward a man standing near a railing. Let's go and look over the side like he's doing, Momma!"

"Alright, alright, just for a minute." She laughed softly.

When they reached the railing, the medium-height, well-dressed, middle-aged man turned to them and tipped his brown derby hat. "Good afternoon," he offered in a deep Spanish accent.

Liam's mom smiled back at the man and nodded.

"I'm Alberto Rodriguez, from San Quedo."

Her eyes widened. "San Quedo? That's up north. My goodness, you're far from home."

He nodded slowly. "Yes, but not far enough yet. I am getting off in Antigua to settle some business affairs. But that's another story," he cut himself off. "Forgive me, what are your names?"

"I'm Bethanie, and this is my son, Liam."

Liam extended his hand toward the man.

Alberto raised his eyebrows and shook Liam's outstretched hand, appearing genuinely interested in the mother and child. "It's extremely nice to meet you both. Where are you two headed?"

Without hesitation, Liam answered, "We're taking the cruise the whole way through the islands!"

Bethanie added with a hand on his shoulder, "It's his first trip. He's very excited."

"As you should be!" Alberto replied. "I have traveled far and wide, but I still remember my first time on a ship—twenty-two years ago. It was special, and each trip has been special since." The man smiled.

"I want to travel the whole world!" Liam blurted out.

The man shrugged and responded enthusiastically, "Then maybe you will!"

Liam flashed a wide grin.

Alberto concluded, "Well, if you'll excuse me, I think I will turn in for a bit. Seems the ship is about to leave, and it will be quite a while before our first stop. Good day, my friends—I hope to see you again soon." He tipped his hat, turned away, and strolled off.

Liam watched the man walk away then disappear around a corner. "He was nice, Momma."

"Yes, most travelers are. They're excited about the adventures ahead, the people they'll meet, and the new places they'll see. Like us!"

Right then, they felt the ship gently rise and fall as it pulled away from the port. Liam and his mother leaned over the railing to see the city of Santo Domingo retreating.

"Here we go!" she cried out as she held on to her son's outstretched hand.

Liam watched with wide eyes as the ship got farther away, until Santo Domingo was just a speck on the horizon.

Liam pointed at the barely visible port. "Is that where we were?"

"Yes, and we can leave all our troubles there on the shore for a while, don't you think?" She smiled at the boy, and he nodded in agreement.

"Let's go to our room, Momma. I want to see it!" He pulled on his mother's hands, and she followed along, chuckling at his enthusiasm. "Okay, okay, I'm coming!"

When they reached room 7, the young mother placed the brass key into the lock and opened the door slowly. As it was pushed farther by the boy, his eyes became like saucers. "Wow, it's all ours?"

Bethanie put her hands on her son's shoulders and looked into his eyes. "Yes, for seven magical days, my boy."

Liam dove excitedly onto the bed. "It's so big and soft!" He laughed and rolled from side to side.

Then Liam paused and asked, "Which island are you looking the most forward to seeing, Momma?"

Bethanie's gaze turned to the ceiling as if she was imagining all the tropical choices. "Well, let's see. We'll visit four of them, so I would say . . . St. John's."

"St. John's? Oh, I bet it'll be very pretty there." Liam smiled and propped up his elbows on the bed as his mom continued.

"Yes, I think it will be a spectacular place. I have seen pictures of the beautiful flowers and the lush landscape . . . like a fairy tale." She held her hands up and together like a ballerina, twirling and grinning.

Liam stood on the bed and drew an imaginary sword from its sheath. "Yes, and I will be the prince who slays the dragon for the fair maiden, Princess Bethanie!"

She giggled, then reached out and tickled her son in the ribs. "Yes, Prince Liam the Protector. I will certainly need to be protected from all the fierceness outside the castle walls!"

She hugged him tightly. As she continued to hold the boy, a tear rolled softly down her cheek, landing on Liam's back.

Sensing the drop, he pulled away to offer her a reassuring smile. "It's going to be okay, Momma. I promise."

As he pulled closer to her, she softly agreed, "Yes, my son, I know you are right. It will . . ."

But, she thought to herself . . . *when?*

CHAPTER 3

After ordering scrumptious room service for dinner, and then getting a good night's rest, the pair woke up and got ready for breakfast.

Once Liam had made the bed, they both looked around the room to make sure everything was in order. "Nice job, Son. As a housekeeper myself, it is greatly appreciated when people keep their quarters organized, so we must always do our best."

Liam nodded.

She smiled, put her hand on his shoulder, and guided him out the door and downstairs for their first breakfast of the trip.

Walking into the dining room, Liam looked around at all the passengers enjoying their meals. "How many people are on our ship, Momma?"

"I was told there are one hundred," she replied. "It's a small ship, and I chose it that way on purpose. It's less crowded and less overwhelming."

They walked up to the hostess. "Two, please," Bethanie volunteered with a warm smile.

"Very good, Señora." The young woman led them to a table off to the side of the buffet and pulled the chairs back gently for each of the two passengers. "Please, have a seat. Your server will be here in just a moment."

The travelers sat down and took in their surroundings. "So much food!" Liam marveled, his eyes glued to the buffet table.

His mother nodded. "Yes, there is plenty, and I have a feeling it will all be quite tasty, but take only what you will eat."

At that moment, a young server with beautiful ebony skin and wearing a freshly pressed white shirt approached. With a sweeping gesture, he offered, "Please, help yourself. There is fresh coffee and orange juice at either end of the buffet. I will return shortly to see if there is anything I can do to be of service."

Liam and his mother stood and walked over to the serving line. As they approached each delectable item, Liam made sure he did as his mom had requested, taking only a small serving of each dish he chose. "We can always go back," she had reminded him, "but we don't want to waste food. There are so many people in our country who have nothing to eat, and we must be mindful of taking only what we will consume."

The two exited the line and returned to their table, and as they sat down, they saw Alberto Rodriguez walking toward them.

"Good morning, friends. How was your night?"

Bethanie nodded. "Good morning, Mr. Rodriguez, it . . ."

He smiled and held up a hand to stop her. "Please, call me Alberto."

Bethanie smiled back and responded politely, "Very well, Alberto. Our night was pleasant—I hope yours was too."

He nodded. "Yes, gratefully. I slept like a baby."

Liam grinned and blurted out, "Would you like to have breakfast with us?"

The man was taken aback, but clearly interested as he glanced at Liam's mom to gauge her response. She motioned toward the empty chair at the table. "Of course. It appears there is a place just for you!"

"Thank you very much," he replied in approval, tipping his derby hat. "I think I'll just have coffee this morning, so I'll get that and be right back." He picked up a mug from the table, then turned and walked to the end of the buffet.

Bethanie leaned over and whispered, "Liam, you shouldn't be so forward. What if he already had plans?"

Liam chuckled. "He *did* have plans, I think—to sit with us."

His mother narrowed her eyes at the boy, then laughed. "Okay, Liam the Great, I'll let it slide this time. Besides, he does seem like a kind person."

Liam speared a bite of sausage and then raised an eyebrow at his mother. "Plus, he seems to be about your age." He laughed and covered his mouth as she shook her head and rolled her eyes playfully.

An approaching voice said, "Well, it is certainly my good fortune to get to join you two today. I am honored."

The young woman blushed. "Thank you, Alberto. It is our pleasure."

Taking a sip of coffee, she added, "You look familiar, Alberto. Have you always lived in San Quedo?"

He shrugged and the corners of his mouth turned up. "People say I have a familiar look. I'm not sure if that's a good thing or a bad thing. I've moved around a good bit, but I'm originally from Santa Guaro, not too far from Santo Domingo."

She cocked an eyebrow. "Ah, that's cocoa country. Are you a farmer? You don't appear to be, if I may say so."

He shrugged. "Yes, I suppose you could say I'm a farmer. How do you know about Santa Guaro?" he asked with a raised brow.

Before Bethanie could reply, Liam jumped in. "It's where my father's from," he added proudly.

Alberto turned his head and smiled knowingly. "Ah, your father is from Santa Guaro, very interesting."

Wanting to head off a potentially uncomfortable ending to the conversation, Bethanie quickly cut in. "Yes, his name is—was—Ernesto. Ernesto Pérez."

There was a notable hesitation in his manner, and then Alberto nodded and spoke. "His name sounds, um, familiar," he offered vaguely.

"He was a hero in the Caribbean War," Liam piled on.

Bethanie reached over and patted Liam's hand, then turned to Alberto. "Liam gets very excited talking about his father. Ernesto was a wonderful man, and we miss him."

"Of course."

Alberto calmly took another sip of coffee, then Bethanie inquired, "And your wife, is she on board?"

Alberto waved a dismissive hand. "I have never been married. I'm certainly not opposed to it, but I haven't met the right woman, I guess." He shrugged.

Liam continued to scarf down his food until the plate was clean. He set down his knife and fork with a loud clank.

Startled, Bethanie turned to her son. "Liam, that was quite the clatter!"

He leaned back, rubbed his stomach, and grinned. "Ah, sorry, Momma. That was my last bite—I'm full."

Alberto noted the time on his watch and took one more sip of coffee. He turned toward Bethanie and said, "I am afraid I must leave. I have an important phone call in ten minutes, and I'll need to do a few things to prepare for it."

Liam and his mother nodded in unison as she replied, "Thank you for joining us, Alberto. It was a pleasure."

He reached out, clasped the woman's hand, kissed the back of it, then crossed his heart in the Dominican gesture of sincerity. "The pleasure was mine."

With that, the gentleman laid down a gratuity, pushed his chair away from the table, then stood and exited the dining hall.

"Momma, he is so nice!" Liam couldn't help reacting excitedly after having such an enjoyable conversation. Bethanie realized it had been a long time since either of them had enjoyed a gentleman's company at a meal—or at any time.

She shrugged her shoulders, then leaned forward and tapped the boy playfully on the tip of his nose. "Yes, I suppose he was. Now, we should be getting on our way, too."

Liam smiled slyly. "You *do* think he was nice, don't you?"

She wagged a finger at him playfully. "He was . . . nice. That's all. Got it?"

Liam laughed. "Got it," he said with a mock salute.

Bethanie placed an additional tip on the table, then they both stood and headed back to the deck where they could look out over the passing sea.

Pointing to an island coming into view, she surmised, "I think that's our first stop, Son—Jamaica."

Liam rubbed his hands together in anticipation. "Sounds like a great place to me—but then again, every place sounds great to me." He chuckled.

As the sea breeze blew through their hair, the young mother put an arm around her boy, and he leaned his head on her side. "I love you so much, Momma. Thank you for bringing me."

She looked tenderly into his big, brown eyes. "I think I should be the one to thank *you*—for being my son." Liam hugged her side tightly, and the two watched as the sun continued to rise above the Jamaican landmass.

After a few moments, she clutched his shoulders and said, "Now, let's go get ready for our day. A little island time is going to be just what the doctor ordered!" The pair turned and headed back to their room.

Right then, the captain's voice echoed through the ship's intercom, announcing their arrival into the Jamaican harbor of Kingston. Immediately, the air was filled with squealing and chattering about the famous destination.

Hearing the captain's words motivated Liam and Bethanie even more, and it wasn't long before the pair was already back on deck with their necessities: a camera, sunscreen, and plenty of water for the hot day ahead.

As they reached the top of the gangplank to disembark, Liam stopped, grabbed his mother's hand, and took a visibly deep breath. The excited boy then turned and shouted out to the vast sea, "Ready or not, Jamaica, here we come!"

The afternoon in Kingston came and went quickly. There were all sorts of historical sights to visit, and Bethanie had already researched the city, so she was able to share her knowledge of the island with her young son, who soaked it all up.

After a lunch of local fish and rice at a small roadside café, the two began their short walk back to the docks. As they approached the cruise ship, they saw Alberto Rodriguez at the top of the gangplank, talking excitedly to the captain. The men shook hands, and Alberto walked away, tipping his hat.

When Liam and Bethanie reached him, the captain waved a hand in greeting. "Welcome back aboard! I'm Captain Diaz—how was your day?" he asked.

"It was great!" Liam gushed. "We went to the Bob Marley Museum. I love reggae."

The captain grinned broadly and then leaned down and whispered into Liam's ear. "I'll tell you a little secret . . . Bob Marley is one of my favorites!"

Liam's face lit up as he turned to his mom, who had overheard the words. "Mom, he loves Bob Marley, too!"

The woman smiled knowingly, then glanced at the man and nodded her approval.

As Liam and his mom began to walk away, Captain Diaz added, "Oh, Mrs. Pérez, I am having dinner with Alberto Rodriguez this evening in the Captain's restaurant. He asked if you and Liam might join us—it will be early, as to accommodate schedules. Say, six o'clock?"

At a loss for words, Bethanie tilted her head and raised her eyebrows at Liam.

"Yes!" he cried, bobbing his head excitedly up and down.

Bethanie smiled and crossed her heart. "That would be very special, Captain. Thank you."

The man gave a short bow. "We will look forward to it." Then, noting the time on his watch, he added, "See you in about two hours."

The two walked back to their room and began recounting the day, talking about all the wonderful people they had met so far and the delicious food they had experienced.

"It's already been more than I could have hoped for, Momma."

She nodded and rubbed Liam's shoulders. "I think the fun is just beginning. Now let's get cleaned up and dressed for our dinner tonight. We must look our best for this memorable meal."

Liam smiled and then marched into the bathroom to get ready as his mother walked to the closet to choose the perfect dress for the big night.

Little did the two know, their evening was about to take a turn they could have never imagined . . .

CHAPTER 4

Liam followed his mother into the captain's private dining room. Alberto was already there, speaking with the skipper. As she and Liam entered the room, the men suddenly stopped talking, and the corners of their eyes crinkled as they gazed in admiration at the woman's breathtaking beauty.

"Bethanie," Alberto spoke first to spare the other's momentary lapse in speech, "you look . . . amazing." Her black, full-length cocktail dress hugged her figure perfectly, and the matching high heels accented her toned legs.

It had been a long time since a man had shown her attention. Bethanie's husband had often told her how beautiful she was, and she suddenly longed for that approval once more.

"Thank you so much," she replied appreciatively, trying not to blush.

Alberto added, "And Liam, you are the best-dressed man in the house!"

Liam nervously tugged at his belt to make sure his shirt was tucked snugly into his trousers, which Bethanie had ensured fit him just right.

"Thank you, Sir," he replied with a toothy grin. He then took his right hand and placed it over his heart.

Captain Diaz motioned for the two to be seated to his right at the immaculately set table, and then he gestured for Alberto to sit on his left.

The captain addressed his guests, "Thank you so much for joining me tonight. I am grateful to be able to host each of you, and I look forward to delicious food, great conversation, and wonderful times together tonight and in the days ahead."

With that, he seated himself, and a server came out to offer each of them a piece of freshly baked *casabe*, a Dominican flatbread.

"Captain, this is marvelous," Bethanie cooed.

Alberto was about to add his compliment when a loud crack was heard from outside the room.

The guests exchanged nervous glances, and the captain stood with a puzzled expression on his face. "Excuse me," he said before walking quickly out of the room. Alberto made small talk with the two other guests as they all waited for an explanation for the noise.

When Captain Diaz returned, he massaged the back of his neck and managed a half smile. "That was quite odd," he said nervously. "But, then again, the sea and its vessels are full of oddness, so you never know," he added with a mirthless laugh. He raised his glass and offered, "To a dinner to remember."

As the group toasted, there was suddenly another loud crack, followed by a massive, almost deafening splintering sound, lasting for several seconds. As the diners turned around in bewilderment, an officer burst into the room. "Captain, there has been a split in the bow!"

Hearing those words, the captain's face went blank, and he replied solemnly, "Sound the alarm. Send the passengers to their designated muster stations."

He gave a pointed look to his officer, who nodded and scurried away.

Bethanie stood, and terror flashed in her eyes as the captain said to his guests, "Lady and gentlemen, I'm not sure what the cause of this problem is, but unfortunately, we must get everyone off the ship . . . *immediately!*"

Grabbing Liam, whose eyes were now like saucers, the young mother turned to Alberto, who simply said, "Come with me."

As he led the way for Bethanie and Liam, they saw crew members running and yelling frantically to get passengers safely into lifeboats. "Everyone to your designated meeting points . . . there are plenty of crafts for all!"

As the trio continued running down the hallway, Liam yelled, "Momma, look!" Their gazes drew to water pouring out from under cabin doors.

Then the panicked voices of passengers reached them. "Help me! Someone *help* me!"

Liam turned toward the voice and saw a woman reaching through her door into the hallway. As he instinctively reached out to assist her, Alberto yelled, "No, Liam!" and he pulled the boy back just as the door burst open and water began cascading into the hallway. The woman came tumbling out in front of the terrified trio.

Alberto stretched out his arm for her, but it was too late—she passed him by in a rush of water.

"Keep moving!" Liam and Bethanie heard him say above the commotion, and they knew they couldn't stay there. As they trudged on, the water began getting higher and higher and was soon up to their waists. Alberto held Bethanie's hand tightly, and Bethanie in turn clasped Liam's hand. Finally, they reached the main deck only to find it in utter chaos. People were attempting to climb clumsily into the primitive-looking lifeboats, and passengers were strapping on life vests as quickly as they could.

All the while, the boat was taking on more water. Clearly, the ship was going down fast . . .

In the confusion, if the captain's muster instructions were heard, they were only marginally followed, as crew members tried desperately to distribute life vests and oversee the onboarding of each craft.

Alberto snatched three vests out of an open closet, which was rapidly filling up with water. He handed one to Bethanie and another to Liam. Strapping the third on himself, Alberto yelled above the fray to the mother and son.

"Put them on quickly, I think I see an open vessel!" He pointed to his left and saw a small lifeboat being put in position for boarding. He scooped Liam up and clutched Bethanie's hand, and the three tumbled into the boat along with two women who fell in at the same time.

"Lower the boat!" the crew member cried out to his partner. At his command, the small vessel began its freefall into the open sea. The screaming of passengers along with the unthinkable sounds of the cruise ship settling slowly into the ocean made it almost impossible to hear anything else as the emergency craft hit the water.

Alberto and Liam grabbed paddles and with all their might, began trying hastily to get the lifeboat away from the massive ship.

Casting a glance out over the choppy water, Alberto caught sight of ten or twelve people thrashing in the waves, trying desperately to reach the safety of a small boat.

He turned quickly away from them and began encouraging the young man. "Good job, Liam! Now, faster, faster!" The two continued to stab at the water, and all five passengers looked on in horror as the lifeboat pulled away, revealing the full picture of the sinking ship.

"This can't be happening!" Bethanie cried as she buried her face in her hands to avoid seeing the impending disaster.

Right then, a wave crashed into the little boat. To the group's horror, Bethanie was flung into the open sea, while Alberto tried to control the vessel.

"Momma!" Liam screamed, dropped the paddle, and lurched forward in a desperate attempt to grab his mother.

With all his might, the boy stretched his thin arms out to her, and his fingers snagged the edge of her soaked vest.

"I have you, Momma—I won't let you go!" he cried out as he valiantly fought to hang on and to keep his eyes open against the stinging sea spray.

Bethanie's eyes were wide as the waves pounded the boat. She felt herself slipping from her son's grasp. . . .

At that moment, Alberto frantically tossed his paddle to one of the other travelers and leapt over to the other side of the boat where Bethanie was fighting for her life. He then lunged to wrap an arm around Liam, as the boy—now barely in the boat—clung to his terrified mother. Painstakingly, Alberto reached out with the other hand and gripped Bethanie, then in one last strained effort, he pulled her back safely into the craft, with Liam maintaining a death grip on her jacket.

The three of them, drenched from head to toe, lay shaking and gasping for breath while the two bleary-eyed women tried to comfort them. As the little boat drifted on the waves, their eyes were drawn to the steadily sinking ship. They saw two more lifeboats full of passengers being lowered from the ship's deck until they hit the water, and then . . .

Silence.

The cruise ship was now totally submerged as the sea claimed the last bit of it. The passengers looked on in disbelief at the spot where moments ago their little slice of oceanic paradise had been floating.

Liam grabbed his mother as they broke down in tears.

The two other passengers instinctively reached over and consoled the mother and son, while Alberto, trembling, craned his neck to see what was happening around them in the darkness. From what he could tell, there were probably a dozen other crafts, each containing five or six passengers at most.

That meant there were likely fifty or so people who had not escaped the ship. The strong, stoic man from earlier now wept openly.

"God rest their souls," he said quietly as he bowed his head.

The survivors were beginning to sound off, letting the others know where they were. They painstakingly paddled their boats toward each other, and after what seemed an eternity, all were circled together on the open sea.

Alberto spoke up loudly. "How many of you have flare guns on your vessel?"

One by one, the passengers from each boat raised their hands.

"Alright, let's not use them all at once. We'll fire off flares one at a time, then spread them out over the next few hours or so if necessary."

Alberto fired the first flare, and it shot into the distance, leaving a trail of bright red in the atmosphere.

Liam looked up in admiration at the man's courage and leadership, but also in terror at what lay ahead for them all.

"Momma . . . what, what will we do?" he stuttered.

"We will wait," she replied exhaustedly.

Liam nodded and squeezed her hand tightly again.

After about thirty minutes, Alberto fired off another flare, his gaze following the trail into the sky.

"It's impossible to tell this time of night where we are. The sky is too cloudy to gain any bearings from the stars, either," he murmured.

Next to him, their fellow passengers began sharing with the group, realizing the awful commonality they now had.

"I am from Colombia," one woman offered.

"I am from Trinidad and Tobago," said the other.

Bethanie introduced herself and Liam but was still in too much shock to carry on a conversation. As Alberto glanced at the other boats, he saw a similar dynamic occurring in each.

"Will we survive, Alberto?" Liam asked in a small voice as the flares continued to go up around him.

Alberto smiled and spoke confidently. "Yes, Liam the Great. You were a hero, and thanks to you, we will *all* survive, and God will be with us."

Bethanie held tightly onto her son and smiled as the other passengers nodded at the words.

"It's true, Liam," his mother added. Then she turned to Alberto. "Both of you were heroes. I am grateful beyond words."

The passengers continued reliving the extraordinary events and making small talk for several hours in the darkness until suddenly, there came a loud cry from one of the other rafts.

"Look!" a middle-aged woman shouted, pointing at the horizon.

Everyone turned their heads to hear the choppy sound of helicopters approaching as their silhouettes against the night sky became clearer.

Cheers rose up from the boats as the maritime survivors waved emphatically at their rescuers.

The helicopters approached one at a time and began lowering crew members down to retrieve the shivering passengers.

"Everyone okay?" The words echoed across the water as the first person was attached to a safety harness. Almost in unison, the passengers announced their miraculously stable conditions with a resounding, "Yes!"

From that point, each person was lifted into an awaiting emergency chopper, and one by one, the rescuers headed safely into the distance.

CHAPTER 5

The helicopter carrying Bethanie, Liam, and Alberto was the last to reach land, just before dawn. Once they arrived, the three passengers walked about thirty steps away from the helipad until they reached a small old red brick building. The entrance was guarded by two soldiers with automatic rifles, and inside was a large, sterile room full of the travelers who had made it off the ship.

"This is just surreal," Bethanie bemoaned as they plopped down in three folding metal chairs in the back of the room. "I could never have imagined. . . ."

A soft-spoken woman in a black-and-white apron approached them with bottles of water and boxed meals complete with baked chicken, roasted potatoes, and peas. The trio immediately began gobbling the food down, as did every other passenger in the room.

A stocky man in a camouflage uniform and a burgundy beret asked for everyone's attention and began reading from a prepared statement. "Ladies and gentlemen, first I want to tell you how grateful we are that each of you survived this horrific event. Fifty-two passengers are missing—including the entire staff—"

Gasps of horror rolled through the crowd.

"—and we are still searching for the cause of this catastrophe. Second, I want to welcome you to the safety of the island of Antigua. We are the closest landmass to where your cruise ship went down, and we will continue to be of assistance in any way possible."

Liam looked at his mom in a puzzled way, and Bethanie returned the gaze, equally surprised. Alberto leaned over and whispered quietly to them both, "Don't worry, you'll be safe here for a while, until we can get back to the Dominican Republic."

Bethanie tilted her head in curiosity as the soldier continued, "As you can imagine, the international press is outside, waiting to talk to you and find out about your experience. I suggest you take your time in speaking with them, but do not feel compelled to tell them anything if you do not want to. Arrangements are being made by the cruise line to put each of you up in a nearby hotel and take care of any interim financial needs you may have. They will also help put you in touch with your embassies."

Liam scrunched up his face, not understanding. His mother patted him on the thigh to assure him that she would explain later.

The soldier concluded, "Now, if you will please remain in this room, some of our representatives will be arriving momentarily to answer any questions you may have."

After what seemed like hours of listening to officials and completing government forms, Bethanie caught a glimpse to her left of two handsome, chocolate-skinned men in dark suits and sunglasses entering a side door. Alberto saw them too, and he immediately stood and began walking toward the inconspicuous entrants. Glancing back at Liam and Bethanie, he said, "Give me just a moment."

As he spoke with the gentlemen, they nodded respectfully, and then Alberto gestured toward his two new Dominican friends. The men followed his point and nodded again, then Alberto motioned for Liam and Bethanie to come over.

As they approached, Alberto said to the attentive men, "These are my friends. I would like them to come with us now, and we will personally get them back to their home in Punta Grande when they are ready."

Alberto noted Bethanie's hesitation, and he explained, "One of my cocoa farms is on Antigua, and I have a home here, also. I would be honored if you would stay with me for a few days until you feel ready to travel. I will make sure you have everything you need in the meantime, and I would be happy to have you both as my guests."

Bethanie looked to Liam, whose smile reassured her, then turned back to the gentleman. "Yes, Alberto, that would be wonderful. Thank you."

With that, he motioned to the two men in suits, then walked over and whispered to the soldier, who bowed respectfully. Alberto gestured to the mother and son to meet him at the side door, and they all exited to be met with a waiting black limousine.

Bethanie was taken aback as they now congregated by the black vehicle. "Well," she said as she put her hands on her hips, "the cocoa business must be pretty good—and you said *one* of your farms is here?" She grinned and shook her head.

Alberto threw back his head and chuckled. "It's a living, anyway! Actually, I was coming back eventually to Antigua on the cruise to finish buying another cocoa farm. The crop has been exceptionally good over the last few years in this part of the Caribbean, so I have been trying to buy up as many farms as I can. Needless to say, I'll probably postpone this purchase for a few days until we, ahem, dry out."

Bethanie smiled, and the chauffeurs helped the three into the limo and took off toward their destination about an hour away.

On the way, Alberto reflected on the boy's heroic actions from earlier. "Liam, I am astounded by the way you handled everything that happened. You were braver at sea than I could have imagined. Were you afraid at all?"

Liam shrugged. "I suppose so. But my father always told me to look fear in the face. So I asked him in my head what I should do, and that's what I heard him say to me—'Face your fear, Liam.'"

Alberto glanced at Bethanie who was smiling proudly at her son and running her fingers through his hair. "It was truly a remarkable event, and you are a remarkable young man."

Alberto nodded. "I must agree. Most grown men would have panicked, but somehow . . . you did not. Your mother is right, Liam. You are a special young man, and you showed that today." He smiled broadly at the weary boy, who politely offered his thanks in return.

After an hour on the highway, the driver turned onto what looked like a long narrow dirt road lined with palm trees as far as the eye could see. "My home is just up there," Alberto said, pointing ahead. "This is my driveway, although it's quite a long one."

Bethanie squinted into the distance. "Yes, it certainly is that."

A minute later, the car pulled up to a gate with an impressive guard post on the right. A fit man in a beige uniform stepped out of the building, and the driver rolled down his window to speak to him. The guard listened intently, then peered into the back of the car and saw the three passengers. He tipped his hat. "Welcome home, Mr. Rodriguez. It has been a long time, and I am so glad to hear you are safe—we were all praying for you."

"Thank you, Carlos," said Alberto. "These are my friends who will be staying in the guesthouse with us for a while."

"Yes indeed, we've been expecting them. Their rooms are ready."

Bethanie cast a curious glance at Alberto and then at Liam, wondering how anyone already knew they were coming to the compound—and how they had time to prepare for their arrival.

Alberto motioned to the guard to let them through, and the driver proceeded. As the car pulled onto the main property, Bethanie was shocked by what came into view. There was suddenly so much color—grass, trees, flowers. It was paradise! The view continued for nearly half a mile, and then Alberto pointed to the right.

"There is where the cocoa beans grow."

"Wow," said Liam, "there are so many plants . . . and so many people working!"

Alberto nodded. "Five hundred acres on this farm. Can you imagine how many chocolate bars we could make from all those plants?" He laughed and leaned back as Liam rolled down the window and took in the sights and the smell of the cocoa. The wind blew his dark hair, and Liam smiled.

The limousine turned toward two homes that came in sight. One was a magnificent, sprawling Spanish-style villa. Next to it, separated by a cobblestone walkway, was the guesthouse Alberto had referred to.

It was the same Spanish-style architecture with stucco construction and terracotta roof tiles, and although the building was smaller, it was still dazzling. In addition to the walkway, the two houses were connected by a magnificent courtyard lined with statues and flowing fountains.

As the limo stopped in front of the main home, the driver and his partner stepped out and opened the rear doors to let the passengers in the back exit the vehicle.

Bethanie looked up in awe. "Alberto, I'm overwhelmed—it's all so beautiful! Thank you for your generosity."

Alberto nodded and gestured toward the guest residence. "Allow me to give you a tour of your home away from home."

The trio walked down the cobbled path, and as they reached the door, it was opened from the inside by a woman dressed in a maid uniform. Seeing Alberto and his guests, she flashed a wide smile. "Hello, Mr. Rodriguez! It is such a pleasure to see you and your friends. We watched the news and were all terrified about what happened, and then when we found out you were safe . . . we were so relieved."

"Thank you, Adriana. I am so sad for the many people whose lives were lost, yet I am grateful Liam and Bethanie made it off with me also." He gestured toward his new friends.

Bethanie and Liam smiled, and the young woman curtsied. "We have your accommodations ready. Please follow me."

Alberto trailed a few steps behind Bethanie and Liam who felt their jaws drop as they crossed the threshold. The home was impeccably decorated, with paintings, rugs, and fresh flowers everywhere.

"Please, come this way," Adriana said. The duo followed her first to a large master bedroom where Bethanie saw multiple beautiful outfits lying on the bed along with shoes, jewelry, and a variety of accessories.

She slapped a hand over her mouth. "What, what are these for . . . ?"

Alberto chuckled and then stepped forward. "They are for you, Bethanie. Since you lost everything—as did most people on the ship—the staff took the liberty of getting some things that would make you comfortable . . . hopefully. If you two need anything in addition to what has been purchased, just let Adriana know; she will get whatever you'd like."

While Bethanie continued to gape, Adriana said, "Liam, we have all of your clothes and needs in the next room—in *your* room."

Liam's eyes were like saucers. "*My* room?"

The woman laughed. "Of course! I hear you are Liam the Great, so you must have your own space!"

He beamed.

The group stepped outside the master suite and walked down a short hallway to another large, well-appointed room.

"Here you are, Master Liam. I trust you'll be comfortable," she offered with a sweeping gesture. There was a large bed, two large windows overlooking the cocoa farm, and plenty of clothes lying on the bed and chair next to it.

"I hope we got your size right, Liam," Alberto said with a wink. "If not, we have a tailor who can fix you up quickly." He glanced over at Bethanie. "Same for your attire, of course." He smiled.

With that, he turned and started to walk away, but then he looked back. "If there is anything else you need, you have only to say the word. For now, I am going to the main house to get myself back in order after our long journey. Would you both like to join me for dinner this evening?"

Liam and Bethanie exchanged glances and smiled, then their eyes came back to Alberto. "Of course, we would love that," Bethanie gushed.

"Excellent. Dinner is served at six o'clock in the main house, and breakfast at eight, so feel free to join me any time. Even if I am not available, the meals will be provided during your entire visit."

He continued, "Adriana will escort you over tonight. She has a room just next to this house, and you can call her anytime you need."

The young lady bowed politely to the guests and then followed Alberto out the door.

Bethanie and Liam were left gawking at their new surroundings.

"Momma, I have never seen anything like this place. How did we end up so blessed as to meet Mr. Rodriguez?"

The Dominican woman seemed to take the question to heart. She cocked her head, admired the beautiful home, and responded pensively, "I'm not sure yet, Liam. But I have a feeling there is a reason. A very, very good reason . . ."

CHAPTER 6

Fatigue from their incredible ordeal had overtaken Liam and Bethanie, so they slept for the rest of the day, both waking only about an hour before dinner. After taking long hot showers, they dressed in one of the fine outfits that Alberto's team had provided. Bethanie wore a lovely knee-length red dress, and when she walked over to Liam's room, she saw he had already excitedly put on a well-fitting shorts outfit. He had an attractive pullover, and his combination of red shorts and black shirt perfectly complemented her outfit.

"Well, look at us! We're matched! You read my mind as to what I would wear, I guess," she said with a laugh.

"I do sometimes think I can read your thoughts, Momma," the boy said. "It's odd; ever since Father died, I feel like I know what you're thinking—and what you're feeling—more and more."

Bethanie cupped his chin in her soft hands. "Yes, I know what you mean. Your father had that ability, too. He often seemed to know what I was thinking—and feeling. He could even finish my sentences sometimes. You have so many of his characteristics that it wouldn't surprise me if you *could* read my thoughts."

Liam stroked his mother's hand tenderly.

"Now, if you can read my mind, you'll know I'm thinking we should reach out to Adriana and have her escort us to dinner." She grinned.

However, at that moment there was a knock at the front door. Liam went and opened it to see Adriana waiting to escort them. Liam turned to his mother and said with a sly smile, "I guess I'm not the only one who can read your mind, Momma." The two laughed as the young housekeeper cocked her head and smiled at the inside joke.

"I thought you might both be ready for your escort, so here I am," she said happily. Bethanie and Liam stepped out to let Adriana close the front door to the guesthouse.

As they got started on their way, Adriana called ahead to them, "Just follow the path over to the house. I'm right behind you. When we leave tonight, there will be lights illuminating the way in case it's dark."

Liam and his mother continued the walk to Alberto's home, and they couldn't help but look around at the beautiful surroundings. Everywhere they gazed, there was lushness and beauty.

"How long has Mr. Rodriguez had this farm?" Bethanie asked aloud with interest.

"I'm not sure," Adriana admitted. "I've been here for nine years, and my mother worked in my position before that. Her mother also had the same job. It has been a blessing for our family to be a part of this household. I am guessing the farm has been in Mr. Rodriguez's family for several generations."

Bethanie shook her head in awe. They had reached the main house, and Adriana stepped ahead to open the large oak doors with brass door knockers. She turned and gestured for the two guests to enter. "Here you are, my friends—and there is Mr. Rodriguez." As if on cue, their host walked up to them wearing a beautiful white silk jacket and light blue linen pants. He was the picture of sophistication.

Bethanie tucked a lock of hair behind her ear. "I must say, you look dashing, Alberto."

He offered his thanks and then gestured with open palms to the two of them. "You both look fantastic! I am happy to see that the clothes fit you so well. Bethanie, once again, you are stunning." As before, he took her right hand and kissed it gently, then turned to Liam and added, "You, sir, are a very handsome hero! Please, both of you, come in."

As they entered, a butler approached and gestured for Liam and Bethanie to sit at the large dinner table in the open-space dining room. A magnificent, modern chandelier hung over the cherrywood table, and the entire room was decorated in a Spanish motif.

Grasping his mother's hand tightly, Liam said quietly, "I feel like we are the Prince and Princess in my story from the boat, Momma."

Bethanie grinned. "Me, too."

The two guests were seated first, followed by Mr. Rodriguez, whose butler pulled his chair back and then pushed it forward slowly when the man was comfortably in.

"Are you hungry?" Alberto asked with a knowing smile.

Liam blurted out, "Starving!"

"*Liam!*" his mother blurted out with mild embarrassment.

Alberto held up his hand, "No, I feel the same way! By all means, let's eat!"

Alberto gently clapped his hands together, and suddenly, three waiters appeared carrying dishes with chrome domes. They stood around the guests and lifted the tops, upon which were displayed different types of fish, vegetables, fresh salads, and anything else that one could want.

Liam stared blankly at the different entrees and sides as the adults began serving themselves. Noticing the young boy not partaking, Alberto put down his silverware. "Oh yes, Liam, I assumed fish and vegetables might not be your favorite—because it certainly wasn't mine when I was your age."

Liam raised a curious eyebrow.

Alberto continued, "So . . ." he clapped once more, and a server brought out another dome-topped plate.

When the server raised the lid, there were two juicy hamburgers and a large side of crispy French fries.

Liam's eyes lit up. "Momma, look! It's my favorite!"

Bethanie smiled, shook her head, and turned to their host. "Why am I not surprised? You've thought of everything."

Alberto raised his shoulders and turned his palms up in mock surprise as Liam grinned.

Alberto took a sip of water and then said, "I just want to say that it is such a pleasure to have you both here with me. I am sad about how our circumstances brought us together, but then again, maybe it was fate that drew us close."

Bethanie nodded her agreement and then asked, "Did you always want to be in the family business, Alberto?"

He gave a slight shrug of his shoulders. "When I was young, I always wondered what my life would look like when I got older. When I was twenty, my father asked me to come into the cocoa business with him. I didn't know what I wanted to do then, so I accepted. I worked the farm, and when my father passed away, I was allowed to take it over. Now that I am thirty-five, I have been able to grow the business to include multiple locations throughout the Caribbean. I have also been blessed to meet many people in my travels, but I have to say, you two are most special."

Bethanie pursed her lips and shook her head. "I must admit, I would never have thought a tragic shipwreck could bring us a friend like you, Alberto. But may I ask . . . what has led you to be so helpful to us?"

Alberto paused and then spoke softly. "For now, let's just say that it is God's will. I strongly believe we have been brought together for a reason, and I will share more about my thoughts on that later. But for now, I want you both to simply enjoy your time here and know that my staff and I are fully at your service if you need anything at all."

Bethanie toyed with a lock of hair and tilted her head. "I have never met a person like you, Alberto, and I have never seen a place like this. Are all your farms this . . . nice?"

"Well, I will say this location is my favorite, although the farm in the Dominican Republic is a close second."

Her eyes sparkled in admiration. "How in the world do you keep up with it all?"

Alberto shook his head. "It couldn't be done without my staff. I have almost a hundred workers between the different farms, and I have managers and supervisors that ensure things run smoothly when I am not there."

Liam jumped in. "Could I see the farm tomorrow, Mr. Rodriguez?"

Alberto nodded. "I will give you a full tour tomorrow morning." Then he pivoted and asked, "Liam, do you like sports? You seem like you would."

Liam cast a glance at his mother, then spoke quietly. "My father was a runner. He was a champion back home, and I always wanted to be like him. When he died, I quit running, but down deep, I think I still love it. My school coach said I had the potential to be great, like my dad, but . . . I don't know. My heart is heavy when I think of it now."

Alberto offered compassionately, "The unexpected things in life can lead us in directions we never would have imagined. But sometimes that direction is exactly where we were supposed to end up all along."

"I think I know what you mean. I would say that Momma and I didn't plan on ending up here—but it's a blessing."

Alberto smiled. "You are a wise young man, Liam. Your father would be proud, as any man would be, to have a son like you. One day, you will run again." He winked at the boy, whose eyes lit up.

Bethanie added, "I believe that whatever we want to do in life, God will help us. We simply must take that request to Him and then trust the outcome. Maybe someday Liam will be an athlete like you say. Whatever he does, I will cheer him on."

Her mouth curved into a smile, and Alberto nodded his approval.

The conversation continued throughout the next two hours while the servers brought out even more beautifully prepared dishes. At one point, Liam said to

Alberto, "Mr. Rodriguez, could we have a bit of your chocolate for dessert?

He grinned and looked at his mother who shook her head and laughed.

"My son and his bottomless pit. Forgive him, Alberto."

Alberto laughed. "I don't blame him—I love chocolate too, and I would say we produce the beginnings of the best chocolate in all the world." He added with a shrug, "However, I may be just a little biased."

With that, he clapped his hands one more time, and a server came out with a silver plate full of a variety of chocolates—large, small, dark, milk, all kinds of treats.

"Here you go, Liam. Take your pick." Alberto chuckled.

Liam turned to his mother who nodded her consent. "Yes, yes, go on." She grinned.

Liam reached for a piece of dark chocolate and immediately sank his teeth into the morsel. His eyes grew wide as he chewed, and then he swallowed. "Mr. Rodriguez, I have never tasted anything that good!"

Alberto turned to Bethanie. "Well, let's see what your mom thinks." He gestured toward the tray of sweets. Bethanie picked out a small milk chocolate piece and took a bite. She looked at Alberto and then at Liam, chewed a few more times, and said, "No wonder you loved that. Alberto, this is amazing!"

The host bowed and placed his hand over his heart. "We aim to please. Now, Liam, if you'll excuse us, I have a few things I would like to talk to your mom about. Adriana can take you back to the guesthouse, if that's okay."

Liam nodded and then held up a finger and giggled, looking at his mom. "Could I have one more piece of chocolate before I go?"

Alberto smiled and motioned to Adriana, who brought the tray of chocolates back to the table.

Liam rubbed his hands together in anticipation and excitedly picked out a large morsel of milk chocolate. Before he headed to the door with Adriana, his expression softened. "Thank you, Mr. Rodriguez, and goodnight, Momma."

Alberto waved, and Bethanie blew her son a kiss . . . and the door shut.

When she turned back from the door, Bethanie's expression dulled as she saw Alberto stand and walk toward the large bay window, massaging his neck and then looking out into the evening sky.

"Alberto, what's wrong?"

Silence.

"Alberto . . . are you alright?"

He hesitated, inhaled deeply, and turned to face her with a sober expression.

Sitting down at the table once more, he took both of her hands in his. "Bethanie, there is something I must tell you . . . and it is going to come as quite a shock."

It was at that moment Bethanie Pérez was acutely aware of the silence in the room, and she felt a chill run up her spine as it occurred to her she was thousands of miles away from her home . . . with a man she barely knew.

CHAPTER 7

The young mother began chewing nervously on her bottom lip as Alberto slowly pulled his hands away from hers and leaned back in the chair.

"Bethanie, I knew Ernesto. I knew him very well."

Bethanie trembled. "You knew my husband? But . . . how?"

Alberto stood, put his hands in his pockets, and walked toward the bay window once again. Staring out into the evening, he began his story . . .

"I left the business for a time to join the army during the Caribbean War. As odd as it sounds, even though we were from the same town, we never knew each other then. But when we each joined the army, Ernesto and I met one night in the barracks—and discovered the similarities we had, including our hometown."

Bethanie covered her mouth in disbelief.

"We became closer and closer friends as the war went on. He told me all about you and Liam, but as you know, we were not allowed to send letters home, so I'm sure you never knew about me or our friendship."

She shook her head. "No, I didn't."

Alberto nodded. "I didn't think so. But I saw pictures of you and Liam, and he told me stories of your lives—I felt like I knew you both. As the fighting got worse, we each became convinced that we would not make it out alive. Our Dominican forces were outnumbered in almost every battle."

Tears rolled down Bethanie's cheeks as she thought of her husband and the terror he must have felt every day—terror in fighting, and terror about possibly not making it home to his family.

"One day in a particularly brutal battle, there were only a handful of us left fighting at least fifty enemy soldiers in the jungle. We were fighting as hard as we could, but one by one, our friends were killed by enemy fire. It was in that battle that Ernesto and I made a pact: if either of us made it out alive, we would take care of the other's family."

Alberto paused and put his head in hands, remembering the horrible scene.

"It was a pact we made with sound minds, and we swapped our blood to seal the agreement. Right after we made the pact, Ernesto was hit in the chest by a bullet from a sniper out of our sight—and he began to bleed terribly. With his remaining strength, he reached into his pocket, pulled something out, and handed it to me—it was a picture, but at that time I shoved it in my jacket and kept shooting."

Imagining the scenario, Bethanie broke down and sobbed uncontrollably. Alberto placed his hands on her shoulders and sympathetically shook his head.

"Please . . . continue. I never knew these details," she managed to say.

"At that moment, a battalion of our soldiers arrived and wiped out the enemy forces—it was like a miracle from heaven for the few of us who were left. But it was not soon enough for my friend . . ."

Tears now rolled down Alberto's face as he struggled to continue. "I looked at Ernesto and realized he was gone—and there was nothing I could do."

He then stepped over to a nearby credenza, opened a drawer, and pulled out an old, yellowed photograph. "When we got out of the jungle, I looked at the picture he had given me . . ."

Bethanie's gaze fell on the crumpled photo as Alberto handed it to her with shaking hands.

She covered her mouth in disbelief as she stared at the image. "I remember this so well . . . Liam and I had the picture taken for Ernesto before he left. We wanted him to always keep it with him to know he was in our hearts."

Alberto nodded. "He did keep it with him—wherever he went."

Bethanie's teary gaze rose to meet that of her new friend.

Alberto's expression softened. "Bethanie, I want to ask you something . . ."

The woman cocked her head, eyes glistening.

"I would like to know if you and Liam would consider moving to Santa Guaro with me. You would have your own house—much like here in Antigua. I have a cocoa plantation there as well, so there is plenty of land and plenty of room for you both. You would have no financial concerns, and you each could . . . make a fresh start."

Bethanie dabbed her eyes. "Alberto, that is so kind of you, but . . . I just don't know."

Right then, she sat up straight and scrunched up her face. "So, wait . . . how did we all end up on the ship together? Incredible coincidence?"

Alberto gave a half shrug. "Not totally. For two years, I have been thinking about the best way to propose this idea to you and Liam. I even came to your town twice, but my courage failed before I could talk to you—you might have thought I was crazy." He shook his head and forced a smile.

"Then I found out you were going on this excursion to the islands, and as I told you, I had business in Antigua, so . . ." He hesitated and added, "I thought maybe the perfect opportunity would present itself."

Bethanie raised her eyebrows and managed a slight smile. "I'm not sure I would call it *perfect*."

Alberto rubbed his temples and then said with a gentle laugh, "Well, that's true. But the fact that we all ended up together on this cruise *was* providential, in my opinion. Bonding with you and Liam and seeing him perform the miraculous feats he did . . . it was as if God was saying to me, 'I can't make my plan any clearer to you.'"

Alberto paused and noted the shocked look on the woman's face.

"Bethanie, there is something else . . ."

Her brow furrowed.

"Ernesto also told me that he had a strong intuition Liam would be a great athlete. He truly believed—even though at that time it was surely too early to tell—that Liam would be a runner unlike people had ever seen."

Enthralled, Bethanie listened closely as Alberto continued.

"God had told him that Liam would impact the world through sport, and through the type of person he would become. It was more than simply a proud father speaking, I could tell. It was as if this was a prophecy that had been delivered to him. He believed it . . . and he convinced me also."

Bethanie nodded. "We had talked about it before, but I never knew how adamant he was in this belief."

"Yes, he was adamant. Bethanie, I also want to help Liam train with the best coaches in the Caribbean as he grows—*if* he is interested. Not only that, but I will gladly pay his way through the finest private schools in the Dominican Republic."

Bethanie shook her head. "Alberto, we could never pay you back, we . . ."

Alberto raised his hand to stop her. "You would never have to pay me back. In fact, I would not allow it. Bethanie, I believe Ernesto was right. What I saw that day as the ship was sinking was unlike anything I could imagine. Liam immediately went into action. He never panicked. Plus, when he went after you, his tenacity was unstoppable."

Bethanie smiled. "Yes, he saved my life."

Alberto shrugged. "It's true. In addition to the mental strength, his physical strength in bringing you back to the raft—it was almost . . . superhuman. I knew then there was something in this child the world would gravitate toward. I also realized he would be successful at whatever he put his mind to."

Bethanie leaned back and exhaled loudly. "It's so much to take in, Alberto. I am grateful for your offer. It's like a dream, but . . ."

As if Alberto knew what she was about to say, he broke in. "There are no strings attached to my offer, Bethanie. You and Liam will have your own life, your own place. I will simply be there any time you need my help. Of course, I know you will want to talk this over with Liam first, and I certainly want him to be comfortable with whatever you decide."

She nodded again. "Thank you. This could be the greatest thing that ever happened to us. I'll speak to Liam in the morning."

The pair stood, and Alberto reached over and kindly put his arms around Bethanie. "Whatever you choose, I am happy to help—or to not help. If you two decide that you don't want me in your lives, I will understand. It's just that . . . I promised Ernesto I would look after his family, and it's the first time I believed I could offer my help in a way that made sense."

Bethanie smiled and then slowly pulled away. "I will let you know as soon as I can, Alberto. Thank you again . . . goodnight."

With that, Bethanie walked out of the room and down the cobblestone path to their "home away from home."

As she arrived at the guesthouse, she reached for the doorknob. Before she turned the handle, she suddenly pulled away and looked up at the starry night, saying aloud, "*Thank you, Ernesto . . . thank you.*"

CHAPTER 8

Liam awoke shortly after sunrise, then walked down the hallway and slowly cracked the door open to his mother's room. To his surprise, he saw Bethanie already awake and sitting in a chair, facing the window with the curtains pulled open.

Hearing footsteps, Bethanie turned around, startled to see her son standing just a few feet away. She pulled the boy toward her as they both admired the rising sun and the gorgeous view over the cocoa fields.

"What are you doing up so early, Liam the Great?" She hugged him tightly, but Liam did not reply. "Is something wrong, Son?"

"No, Momma. I just . . ."

"You just what?"

"It sounds so silly but, I had a dream last night that I was walking with Father."

"Ah, I see. Did the dream make you sad?"

To Bethanie's surprise, the boy shook his head. "We were walking together, and we shared so much laughter. Then he said to me, 'Liam, I always want you to live a life full of laughter, do you understand?'"

The boy paused. "Then he said to me, 'There will be times when you are sad, and that's normal. But just remember, if I am ever gone, there will still be so much good left in the world. You must always look for that.'"

Bethanie fought back tears as she said, "What else did your father say?"

"He said there would be people that come into our lives to help us, and we should let them."

Bethanie held her breath. "What else?"

"He said he had always tried to help people, and he knew that I would be the same way. But he also said that it is important to allow people to make a difference for us, too—because it is good for us *and* for them. He said no one can do everything by themselves."

Liam hesitated, noticing a tear rolling down his mother's face.

"Momma, I didn't mean to make you sad."

She shook her head and wiped the tear away with the sleeve of her robe. "No, Liam, these are tears of happiness. Hearing you talk of seeing your father—I could almost hear him saying those exact words."

Liam smiled at her. "Yes, it felt so real."

Bethanie motioned for him to sit down across from her.

"Son, about that dream . . ."

Liam tilted his head in interest as his mother continued. "When your father talked with you about others helping us . . ."

"Yes, Momma?"

"Liam, I found out last night that Mr. Rodriguez knew your father."

"What?" The boy's eyes widened.

She nodded. "They were in the war together and became very good friends. They made a promise that if one of them did not survive, the other would help his family. Alberto told your father he would be honored to do that."

"But . . . what does that mean?"

Bethanie took a deep breath. "Liam, Alberto has invited us to come live with him in Santa Guaro. He has another cocoa plantation there with a home and a guesthouse like this one. We would be free to live our lives, but he would help us anytime we needed it. He will also pay for you to go to a private school—the finest in the Dominican Republic—and if you decide to play sports, he will help us pay for coaches."

Bethanie let Liam take in the news in silence before saying, "Liam, we do not have to say yes. I can . . ."

Liam shook his head and smiled. "Momma, this is what Father talked to me about in my dream. Don't you see?"

Bethanie leaned back as Liam continued, "He wanted us to be happy. He wanted us to make sure that we not only helped others, but we let others help us. Momma, you have left your job, so going to a new town isn't a problem. I want to go to a new school! I've had enough of the other children knowing the pain I have dealt with—and being teased for not having a father. Maybe a new start is exactly what we need."

Bethanie leaned forward and hugged her son, tears now streaming down her face. "Yes, my sweet son, I believe you are right."

She pulled back from him and looked deeply into his eyes. "Liam, your father would be so proud of you. He always—*we* always—have known you are special. Your wise words once again confirm it. I promise I will make sure your life is the best it can be. I also trust that Alberto has our best interest at heart, and I believe there will be great opportunities ahead for us."

She rubbed her son's head and wiped her tears away once more.

"Why don't we tell Mr. Rodriquez about our decision at breakfast? He will be thrilled to know he can help us—and honor your father's wishes."

Liam nodded and smiled, then stood and embraced his mother tightly as they looked together over the acres of cocoa fields at the clear blue sky and now fully risen sun . . .

When Bethanie and Liam arrived at breakfast, they found Alberto sitting with a book and a cup of coffee. As the pair approached the table, he put down the book and stood.

"Ah, my guests are here. Suddenly my day is getting even better!" He gestured toward two of the chairs, and Bethanie sat down, followed by Liam.

As Alberto took his seat once more, a server arrived and asked the two for their breakfast order. Liam rubbed his hands together eagerly. "I would like some cereal please—with milk and strawberries."

The server nodded and raised her eyebrows inquisitively at Bethanie. "And you, ma'am?"

"Just yogurt and some orange juice, please."

"Of course." She bowed and strolled away toward the kitchen, leaving the trio at the table.

"How was your night?" Alberto asked with a smile.

"Oh, I think we both slept well. In fact, Liam even had a good dream about his father."

Liam nodded at his mother.

"Alberto, I have talked with Liam about your generous proposal . . ." She paused.

Alberto straightened noticeably in his seat.

"We have decided to accept your offer, and we are incredibly grateful for the opportunity."

The man stood once more and clapped. "This is wonderful news! I am so happy for the opportunity to have you both in my life—and to help in any way possible."

Alberto turned to Liam. "I know your father is looking down, smiling and feeling very proud."

Liam's lips turned up, and then the three began chatting excitedly about logistics.

"I will have any items you might need from Punta Grande shipped as soon as possible to my home in Santa Guaro. I suggest, if I may, that you keep your current home for a while. You may need to be there at times, and when you are not, I will have people drop by and make sure all is well."

"Thank you," said Bethanie. "This is wonderful, Alberto. I would also like to start looking for a school for Liam as soon as we're able to return to the Dominican Republic. It's only a short time until classes are in session, so hopefully we can still get him into a school where he can excel."

"Agreed," Alberto said with a nod. "We shall leave for the Dominican Republic the day after tomorrow."

"Liam," Alberto asked pensively a moment later, "would you like to go for a run with me in the mornings when we get to the Dominican Republic? Whenever I can, I like to wake up early and get a little exercise in. Maybe you can teach me a thing or two about running?"

Liam smiled. "It would be a pleasure, Sir."

Out of the corner of his eye, Alberto saw Bethanie cast an affectionate glance toward him as she sipped her orange juice. His eyes crinkled in delight.

After breakfast, the pair went with Alberto for a jeep drive around the island. First, they drove around the cocoa fields and saw all the workers busy with their crops. Liam noticed how Alberto always stopped to talk with them, and the boy was amazed at how the owner knew all his staff members by name.

"How do you know them all?" Liam asked with surprise.

Alberto shrugged. "They are not merely workers; I consider them my friends. I am blessed to have them help me with these crops—and I never take that for granted."

Bethanie's lips turned up as she heard these words. She couldn't help but think of her husband. "No wonder you and Ernesto got along so well—you seem to have had a lot in common."

Alberto smiled at the comment as the jeep rounded a curve and headed off the plantation. "That is quite the compliment to be compared to Ernesto—thank you." He winked at Liam, who beamed back.

After a day of traveling around the small island and seeing the many sights Antigua had to offer, the group headed back home and began getting ready for dinner. They met together at six o'clock and sat down to the chef's beautiful Antiguan meal of grilled chicken and seasoned rice.

Alberto commented, "Javier is one of the finest chefs in the Caribbean. It is an honor to have him here with us. I shall miss him when we go to the Dominican Republic."

Bethanie nodded her approval. "Every dish we have had here has been magnificent, Alberto. You must be so proud to have a team that supports you and your business like this."

"Yes indeed, and you will find it is the same in the Dominican Republic." As if that had triggered his memory, he added, "By the way, our flight leaves the day after tomorrow at 11 a.m. Bring what you think you might need, but leave anything extra here for future visits. We will get everything else you want when we reach the Dominican Republic."

Bethanie's mouth curved into a smile. "That sounds perfect."

The trio enjoyed their dinner, then Liam excused himself as he had the previous evening to head back to his room—but not before his nightly piece of chocolate.

Alberto called to the server who brought the large tray of sweets back again. This time, Liam looked at his mother and asked, "How about three of them tonight, Momma? Please?"

She narrowed her eyes and wagged a finger at him. "Alright, if it's okay with Mr. Rodriguez—but three is your limit, young man."

Alberto grinned. "There's plenty to go around, I assure you. Enjoy, Liam."

The boy excitedly took the chocolate and scampered off to his room, leaving his mother alone at the table with Alberto.

"Shall we step out on the balcony? I think the sun has gone down, and the weather should feel very nice tonight."

Bethanie nodded, and a smile danced on her lips as she rose from her chair.

When they walked out on the balcony, Bethanie was taken aback by the view. "Alberto, it is uncanny. Everywhere we go on this property, there is beauty." She pointed into the distance. "The creek, the flowers, the lushness . . . it's all spectacular."

"I'm glad you approve," he grinned. Then he added gently, "Bethanie, I have to say, just the time we have spent together so far, I feel so close to you and Liam. I never would have dreamed it."

She turned her eyes away, then returned her gaze to Alberto. "Yes, I agree. Sometimes I wonder about God's plans. I should never doubt, but I must say, the last few years have been so difficult. Having met you and being part of this with Liam . . . it's a gift. Thank you again."

Alberto looked softly into her eyes. "It is . . . my pleasure." Then as if he caught himself becoming emotional, he glanced at his watch and said to Bethanie, "Ah, it's late. You need to get some rest. There will be lots to do tomorrow to get ready to go the next day."

Bethanie suddenly felt butterflies in her stomach, wondering what the days ahead in the Dominican Republic would hold. It all was happening so fast. . . .

CHAPTER 9

When their departure day arrived, Bethanie awoke early. In the dim light of her room, she began putting items in the two suitcases that Alberto had provided for her and Liam. It seemed strange and sudden, she thought, to actually be going through with this. On the one hand, it was a dream come true, but on the other hand, she was aware she was starting a new life in a new home, with a new person involved.

Bethanie brushed her nervous thoughts aside and continued packing. When she was done gathering the most important items, she went into Liam's room and saw him sleeping soundly. As she gazed at her little boy, she realized she would do anything to spare him from the pain he had felt after the death of his dad. Then it occurred to her that stepping out of her comfort zone with Alberto was indeed the right thing to do . . . for Liam. He would have opportunities she would never have been able to provide for him.

Plus, he would have a father figure—something she knew he desperately needed now and in the future.

Right then, Liam rolled over and saw his mom standing over his bed. "Momma, are you okay? What's wrong?" A look of fear swept across his face, causing Bethanie to reach down and gently touch his cheek.

"Nothing, my son. Everything is fine. I just wanted to come in and wake you so we would be on time . . . today is the day we leave for home." She smiled reassuringly.

Liam reached up and grabbed his mother with both arms. "Momma, I think this is going to be a very good thing for us." Seeing the smile on her son's face gave Bethanie the courage she needed at that moment.

"You're right, Liam. I know that your father would only want the best for us. For him to have asked his friend to support us, well, Mr. Rodriguez must surely be a special person."

Liam agreed and then stretched as his mother pulled back the covers.

"When you're ready, start putting a few things on the floor near the door, if you would like to take them back home. I will pack them for you after breakfast."

Liam nodded.

"I'll come back in a bit, and we can go down to breakfast together. Alberto is going to join us, and then he will have someone take us to the airport."

With that, Liam sprang out of bed and began the task of deciding which items he would take on his journey as his mother went back to her room to get ready for the morning meal.

After about half an hour, Bethanie returned and knocked on Liam's closed door. When he opened it, to her surprise, he already had his items neatly put in a pile, ready to be packed. He was also fully dressed, ready for his day, even having made up his bed.

"Wow, you did good, Son. I have to say, when I was your age, I was a little bit slower in getting my chores done. You . . . are *fast!*"

Liam smiled broadly, and his mother took what she could from the pile back to her room to put them in the suitcase. As she turned to go back for the next load, there was Liam, arms full.

"Here you go, Momma, I think that's it."

Bethanie took the rest from him, then put everything in the suitcase and zipped it up. "Okay, I think we're ready," she beamed. "Let's head over to the house and have some breakfast—we have a big day ahead!"

The pair walked out of the guesthouse and down the now familiar cobblestone path.

When they arrived, Liam stepped ahead of his mother and grinned as he knocked on the large door. Bethanie rubbed his head and smiled as Adriana opened the door to welcome them.

"I thought you might have been asleep, Adriana, so we did not want to bother you for an escort."

Adriana chuckled. "Oh, we don't sleep late around here, ma'am, there's too much to do!"

Right then, the door was pulled wide, and Alberto appeared, grinning. "The travelers are here!" He clapped his hands together and reached out to hug Liam before doing the same for Bethanie. "Come in!"

The pair entered, and Adriana shut the door behind them as Alberto gestured toward the table. It was again already set and full of delicious breakfast foods, including the hearty Antiguan breakfast staples of fungee, pepper pot, and black pudding.

"There is a little bit of everything this morning. Chef Javier wanted to not only send you off in style with a local meal, but he also wanted us to be able to take a few items on the flight in case we got hungry. My favorite are the muffins," he added, pointing at the tasty blueberry muffins in a basket.

"It all looks wonderful. My compliments to the chef—again," Bethanie said.

As the three sat and began their breakfast, Alberto took a sip of coffee and turned to Liam. "Well, my friend, it's a big day. Are you ready?"

Liam nodded his head. "Yes, Sir, I am!"

Bethanie's eyes twinkled as she glanced at their host, who added enthusiastically, "Okay, then, let's dig in, and we will head to the airport as soon as we finish!"

They gobbled down their breakfast then headed back to their rooms to double-check that they had remembered to pack everything important. When they were satisfied that they hadn't forgotten anything in their suitcases, Bethanie called for Adriana, who returned with a staff member to take their luggage to the car.

As they all walked together, Adriana said softly, "I will miss you both. It has been such a pleasure to have you with us." Then she paused and added, "I don't think I have seen Mr. Rodriguez this happy in years—maybe ever."

Liam looked up at his mother, and a smile crossed her face as she placed her hand across her heart. "Thank you, Adriana. Our stay with you all has been a gift— and we look forward to seeing you on our next trip here . . . hopefully very soon." She reached out and gently embraced the young woman.

As the group reached the front of the house, they saw Alberto standing with a driver and three suitcases. Alberto motioned to the driver to grab their bags, which he did, placing them in the back of the shiny black limousine and then taking Alberto's luggage and doing the same.

"Well, friends, the time has come. A new life lies ahead. Shall we go?"

Liam and his mother exchanged smiles, and with one more wave to Adriana, the two jumped into the back of the waiting car. Alberto stepped inside the passenger's side of the vehicle, whereupon the driver closed each of the doors, then walked around and started the vehicle.

"I think you know the route, my good man." Alberto smiled and placed a gentle hand on the driver's shoulder.

"Yes, sir." The car pulled away gradually until the beautiful house was a distant speck.

After a few moments, Bethanie leaned up to Alberto and asked nervously. "I know this sounds foolish, but . . . you do have our tickets, right?"

Alberto paused, then playfully hit his forehead with his palm. "I knew I forgot something!"

Seeing the look on Bethanie's face, he laughed and then touched her hand reassuringly. "We won't need tickets."

The woman scrunched up her face in confusion.

"We are taking my plane," he replied with a grin.

Liam, overhearing the conversation, broke into a wide grin and extended his arms into the air with clenched fists. "Woo-hoo!"

Bethanie put her head in her hands and smiled. "Oh my gosh, I thought . . ."

"Relax, it is all taken care of, Bethanie. We will be at the airport in fifteen minutes, then we will be in the air on the way back to the Dominican Republic soon after."

Bethanie leaned back in relief as the limousine took them closer to their destination.

Once the trio arrived at the small jetport, the driver set their luggage by the waiting plane. As if on cue, a middle-aged, dark-skinned man in a pilot's uniform stepped out and tipped his hat. "Welcome, everyone. We should be taking off in about ten minutes. I'll get your luggage on board."

As the barrel-chested man started to pick up the suitcases, he reached out and shook Alberto's outstretched hand. "Great to see you again, Mr. Rodriguez—especially after the ship incident—you scared us all to death." The man grimaced and shook his head.

Alberto nodded. "Yes, I think it may be a while until I take a boat anywhere again, Marcos. The air is my new favorite method of travel." He laughed.

Once all the luggage was on the plane, Alberto looked back at the limousine driver and waved goodbye, then stepped up the stairs to join his group. When he was inside, he introduced Bethanie and Liam to the flight attendant, a tall, lanky Antiguan named Joseph, and then the pilot closed the door.

Before he walked toward the front of the plane, the pilot told his passengers, "We should be in Santo Domingo in about an hour. We'll make it as smooth and easy a ride as possible, but go ahead and buckle up, and we will be on our way."

As the three passengers tightened their belts, they felt the plane begin taxiing down the runway. Liam glued himself to the window as the aircraft picked up speed and then lifted off the ground.

The young boy and his mother exchanged broad smiles, knowing their lives were about to change for the better. . . .

CHAPTER 10

The flight was short and uneventful, although Alberto entertained the group with stories of the cocoa business, life in the army, and some wonderful narratives of his times with Liam's father. The boy was mesmerized, and each time Ernesto was mentioned in a tale, Liam's chest seemed to puff.

Then, an hour later, the jet began its descent, and the pilot reminded the passengers to fasten their seatbelts while Joseph came around one last time to collect their leftover cups and napkins.

As the aircraft smoothly landed and taxied in, the pilot announced over the intercom, "Welcome home to the Dominican Republic!"

Upon hearing that, Bethanie squeezed her young son's hand, and her lips turned up into a broad smile. Liam stared excitedly out the window as the plane slowed to a stop amidst the background of Dominican palm trees.

The pilot then opened the door and extended the aircraft's stairs. Each person stepped off slowly, and as Liam and his mother exited, they seemed to relish the smell and feel of being back in their homeland.

At that moment, an extremely dark-skinned man of average height, sporting a brown suit and dark sunglasses, approached the group. "Welcome to the Dominican Republic, everyone. I am Juan, your driver. I will get you back to Mr. Rodriguez's home."

"*Our* home," Alberto corrected the man gently. "It also now belongs to my friends Liam and Bethanie." He smiled, and the driver tipped his hat.

"Yes, sir." Juan grinned, then reached down and picked up the suitcases that Joseph had set by the sleek, black SUV before opening the car doors for his guests.

The three passengers piled into the limo, with Liam and his mother sitting in the back, and Alberto once again in the front passenger seat. While strapping himself in, he looked back at Bethanie. "By the way, if you'll give me your keys and tell me where your car is in the parking lot, I will have someone bring it to the house. The port is not too far from here."

She shook her head and grinned as she handed him the keys. "You've thought of everything, Alberto. I keep forgetting my car has been in that parking lot since before we left for the cruise. It seems like months ago!"

The driver joined the passengers. Starting the vehicle, he glanced over at Alberto, looked in the mirror at his guests, and then put the vehicle in gear to begin the short journey to the cocoa farm.

Along the way, the group admired the passing tropical scenery. "It's interesting how different the landscape is in the Dominican Republic compared to Antigua, even though the islands are so close to each other, isn't it?" Bethanie remarked.

Alberto nodded. "It's also a much different business climate here, compared to Antigua. There are so many more rules and regulations to deal with."

Not long after, the driver turned the car off the highway and onto a small dirt road like the one that led to Alberto's home in Antigua. "We're almost there, everyone," he said with a smile.

In another minute, the car reached the Rodriguez farm, and just like in Antigua, there was a gate which provided security for the property. The limousine pulled up to the small guard shack, and a man in a khaki uniform stepped out to greet the vehicle.

When the guard recognized Alberto, his eyes lit up. "Mr. Rodriguez! I am so happy to see you again—welcome home!"

"It is a pleasure to be here, Manuel," Alberto returned. "It's also a pleasure to see *you* again. You are looking good—lost a little weight, I think?" Alberto grinned and raised an eyebrow.

"Yes, sir! I am trying to stay away from the *cerveza*, but it is hard." The guard laughed as he rubbed his stomach.

"Well, keep up the good work—you're making progress. All the women in Punta Grande are going to be after you soon!"

The staff member threw back his head and laughed deeply, then raised the gate and saluted as the vehicle cruised into the compound.

Bethanie lowered the window and gazed out at her surroundings. Liam leaned over his mother and peeked out, too. "It's a beautiful farm, just like the one in Antigua, Mr. Rodriguez," the young boy said.

Alberto nodded. "Yes, the more I think about it, *this* one might be my favorite." Laughing, he added, "But don't tell the farmers I said that—they will get cocky."

Liam chuckled.

Bethanie pointed at a few dogs roaming the grounds, and she wondered aloud, "Do you have many animals here?"

"Several dogs, also a few cats. I don't know how they ended up here, but I have grown attached to them, so we take care of them and feed them. They seem happy—or at least I've never heard them complain." He smiled slyly.

After another minute, the car pulled up to the residence. Interestingly, the building looked exactly like the one in Antigua. The guesthouse, too, was a mirror image of the one they had left behind earlier that day.

Before Bethanie could comment, Alberto added, "I wanted the houses to be the same. Whenever I visit one of my farms and properties, I like them to feel 'just like home.' So, I had the architect design twin properties." He grinned.

The driver parked the limo in front of the main house, and a young woman around twenty years old stepped outside to greet them, wearing a housekeeper uniform. She curtsied to the group as the chauffeur opened the door and helped each of them exit the vehicle. "Hello, Mr. Rodriguez—and this must be Miss Bethanie and . . . Mr. Liam!"

Liam's eyes became wide. The boy leaned over to his mother and said quietly, "Momma, she knows our names!"

Bethanie smiled, put her arm around her son, and then spoke to the young woman. "Yes, and you are . . . ?"

"I am Eliza. It's nice to meet you all. I have heard so much about you."

Bethanie bowed her head humbly and crossed her heart with her right hand. "Thank you, Eliza. We look forward to being here."

The staff member flashed a warm smile. "The pleasure is truly ours. May I interest you in anything to eat?"

Bethanie waved a hand. "Thank you, but we have packed lunches which the chef in Antigua thoughtfully prepared for us. The flight was so fast, we never opened them, so we'll be fine."

Eliza looked at Alberto and asked politely, "Shall I show them to their house?"

Alberto nodded. "Please do." Then he turned to Bethanie and added, "We'll have your luggage brought to your rooms shortly. I am going to the main house to freshen up a bit and return a few phone calls. I will check in on you later—and again, shall we have dinner—at six?"

Bethanie rubbed her chin and responded, "This seems very familiar—and the answer is yes." She grinned.

Eliza brought the group into the guesthouse and beamed as they entered. "Of course, you are familiar with the house—since it is just like the one in Antigua, I understand."

"Yes, it appears to be," said Bethanie. "That home was lovely also."

Eliza then gestured off the living room to the kitchen. "If you will tell us how you would like your refrigerator stocked, we will get that taken care of as soon as possible."

Noting Bethanie's surprise, the young worker explained, "Mr. Rodriguez insisted that there should be no expense spared for you two. So, that's the way it will be." She pointed a playful finger at Bethanie. "When Mr. Rodriguez insists, he is hard to argue with."

She laughed, and Bethanie smiled. "I have come to see that."

Eliza then turned to Liam and added, "Let's take you to your room. I believe they call you 'Liam the Great,' correct?"

She grinned and Liam laughed. "Yes, ma'am."

Eliza gave the boy a quick tour and then escorted him back to his mother. "I live on the grounds, so if I can help either of you, please just ring me, and I will come right away. Welcome to your new home." With that, Eliza turned and walked out the door, leaving Bethanie and Liam alone in their new quarters.

"Well, here we are, Son. Back home . . . sort of."

She laughed, and Liam chimed in, "Yes, and it's great to be back on our island, Momma. When can we go back to the house in Punta Grande and pick up our things?"

Bethanie cocked her head in thought. "We'll figure that out. Maybe tomorrow. For now, how about we take a walk on the property and explore for a few minutes? We don't have our sneakers since we don't have our luggage yet, but these shoes should be okay for a short walk."

Liam nodded.

The two stepped back outside into the Dominican Republic heat and immediately felt themselves beginning to perspire. "Wow, we definitely are home, Momma!" Liam said as he wiped the beads of sweat off his brow.

As they walked around the property, they saw many similarities to the farm in Antigua. Indeed, it seemed as if not just the buildings, but the entire land was designed the same.

"Let's walk this way," Bethanie said, pointing toward a creek near the acres of crops.

As they walked, Liam asked, "Momma, do you *really* like Mr. Rodriguez?"

Bethanie began swinging their arms together and she grinned. "Do *you*?"

Liam looked ahead as if he was thinking. "Yes, he's been so nice to us. I do think Father would be happy with our being here."

Bethanie looked approvingly at Liam. "I think you're right." Changing the subject, she gestured at the creek, which was now only a few yards away. "Let's go throw a few rocks in the creek—like we used to with your father."

Liam excitedly ran the distance to the creek and picked up some rocks for both of them. Bethanie followed behind, but suddenly, she lost her footing on the uneven ground and started to fall.

Seeing that, Liam yelled, "Momma!" as the woman regained her balance just in time.

"That was close—better be careful down here when you're not wearing the right shoes," she added in a nervous voice.

Liam offered his hand to his mother, pulling her safely next to him. He handed several rocks to her.

Bethanie glanced at Liam and then said, "Remember, when you throw a rock in, you must make a wish every time."

Liam nodded. "Yes, I definitely remember that, Momma." He took a small stone, closed his eyes, and then after a short pause, opened them and tossed the rock into the water.

"So, what was your wish?"

Liam shook his head. "Momma, you know I can't tell you that—then it wouldn't come true!"

She shrugged. "Ah yes, I forgot the rules. How silly of me." Bethanie laughed, shut her eyes tightly, then opened them and flung one of her rocks far across the creek.

"Wow, Momma, you've gotten strong!"

She chuckled. "Well, I have a strong son—I can't let him leave me behind too quickly!"

After a few more throws, the pair headed back to the house. Bethanie glanced at her watch. "I suppose we can rest for a little while, then we can start getting ready for dinner."

"I wonder if the food is as good here as it is in Antigua," Liam said.

"Young man, I'll tell you this . . . if I don't have to cook it, the meal will be wonderful no matter what it is!"

Bethanie laughed, putting an arm around her smiling son, and the two headed home.

CHAPTER 11

When six o'clock came, Liam and Bethanie walked over to the main house to meet Alberto for dinner. The large door opened as they approached, and a tall, distinguished gentleman in butler attire appeared. "Good evening, Liam and Miss Bethanie, and welcome home! I am Thomas. Mr. Rodriguez is waiting for you in the den."

He bowed as the pair entered, and then he gestured toward the den. Walking inside, they spotted Alberto standing, looking out a bay window. Hearing them enter, he turned.

"Welcome again!" he said with open arms. "Can I get either of you anything before dinner? Bethanie, may I interest you in a glass of wine?"

"That would be wonderful." She turned to Liam. "How about some water for you?"

Liam nodded. Within seconds, Thomas brought back two glasses of white wine and a small bottle of water, then presented a drink to each person.

Alberto held up his glass and said, "To the Pérez family and the good times in the Dominican Republic," to which they raised their drinks and toasted. After a few minutes of sipping their beverages and chatting, they headed to the dining room.

The meal once again was perfect, as was everything in the home. About halfway through dinner, Alberto turned to Liam and offered, "How about you and I take a little jog in the morning like we talked about back in Antigua? I am ready to get back on an exercise program, and maybe you can motivate me."

Liam looked over at his mother. Seeing the hesitation on his face, she gently said, "Liam, I think it is time for you to try running again. You loved it so much—and I'll bet you could teach Mr. Rodriguez a thing or two to help him." She turned and winked inconspicuously at Alberto.

Liam was quiet for a moment as he considered the offer. "Yes, I think I would like to try it. Although . . ." his voice trailed off.

Alberto looked quizzically at the young man who then added, "Although I might be a little rusty."

Alberto rubbed the boy's head. "Well, that is probably better for me so that you don't outrun me too badly." The man grinned broadly and added, "I will meet you tomorrow morning at eight o'clock out on the driveway."

Liam nodded, then turned to his mom and an excited smile swept across his face.

The next morning, Liam woke up a few minutes before eight, jumped out of bed, and immediately walked to the closet to pick out his running shoes. He thought back on the mornings he would lace up his sneakers and go jogging with his dad, and he missed those days so much. It wasn't the running that he missed as much as it was . . . the conversations. It was the words of encouragement and wisdom his father shared with him. After those moments together, Liam always felt ready to conquer the world. He truly did feel then like Liam the Great.

Today he wondered what it would be like—doing this almost sacred activity with someone other than his father. He put on his shorts and shirt, tied his shoes, and quickly brushed his teeth, still thinking of those days.

When he walked out the front door, his mind was still focused on those early mornings with his father, but he was snapped back to the present by the approaching voice of Alberto.

"There's my running mate," he boomed. "I'm hoping you can teach me a thing or two, Liam. It's been a while since I have done any running, and I'm just not sure how it'll go." He winked at the boy.

As Liam regained his focus, he chimed in with, "Well, it looks like you've got the right clothes and shoes on, so that's a good start."

Alberto smiled, then shielded his eyes from the bright sun and surveyed the land. He pointed to the western part of the farm and commented, "Let's start that way and see where it takes us."

Liam nodded, and with a quick pat on the back from Alberto, the pair was off.

After a few minutes of gentle jogging in silence, Alberto looked over at the boy and offered, "Not too bad for an old man, am I?" He laughed, and Liam laughed with him.

Alberto continued, "And how are you feeling, Liam?"

"So far, so good. I'm actually liking this—I wasn't sure . . ." His voice trailed off.

"I understand. Sometimes the best way to rekindle a love for something is to give yourself a little space from it. Whether it's running or dealing with people, a little time apart can help."

The two continued their jog, and Alberto pointed out parts of the farm as they passed by. "There is where some of our staff members bunk in the evening," he said proudly. "They love it here, and I think we've done a good job of making sure every employee is treated well and given what they need to be comfortable."

Liam craned his neck to see the house and its inhabitants.

Right then, two field hands stepped out and Alberto yelled cheerfully, "Hi, Paco! Hi, Eduardo!"

The two men waved and called back, "Careful with your running, Boss. You're not as young as you used to be!" They chuckled, and Alberto laughed with them and shook his head.

After about twenty minutes, Alberto looked over at Liam's effortless stride and commented, "You're not even breaking a sweat!"

The youth's lips turned up into a sly smile. "Maybe a little bit."

Alberto continued, "You used to really love running?"

The boy thought for a few seconds and then replied candidly, "My father made me believe I could be great. His words, and running alongside him, just made it fun. One time I even dreamed I was a world champion." He smiled.

Albert nodded. "Liam, I remember from talking with your father that he believed you had great skill—and great mental toughness. When I saw what you did after your mom fell out of the lifeboat, well, I was astounded. Most people—grown men or otherwise—would have panicked. You simply sprang into action."

Liam cocked his head and listened carefully as Alberto continued, "When a person has great talent, it puts them with a small percentage of people. When a person has great talent *and* great courage *and* mental toughness, it puts them in a class with very, very few people. Just from what I have seen so far, I think you have excellent potential, regardless of what path you choose."

His words struck a chord in Liam—and they felt good. Memories of his father's encouragement came flooding back to him.

"Thank you," Liam beamed.

Alberto wiped the sweat from his brow and pointed toward the house. "What do you say we head back home? I think this senior runner has had enough for today."

Liam agreed, and as the pair began jogging back, Alberto noted they were just about a hundred yards from the house. Raising an eyebrow, he turned to Liam and asked with a grin, "Got any juice left in you?"

Liam matched Alberto's sly look and then turned his gaze resolutely toward the residence as if were the finish line of a great race. Without another word, the boy bolted toward the goal at a speed that shocked Alberto, who stopped in his tracks, put his hands on his hips, and watched in amazement. Within what seemed like mere seconds, Liam was standing in front of the home, with a large grin plastered on his face.

"How was that?" he asked loudly as Alberto approached the house, still staring in awe.

"Liam . . . I can't believe your speed. I think that is the fastest I have ever seen someone run—regardless of age." He shook his head.

"Nah, you're just saying that."

The man shook his head and put his hand on the boy's shoulder affectionately. "No, I assure you, I am not."

Alberto turned back toward where Liam had started the sprint, and then followed the path with his line of sight. "We shall have to try that again tomorrow."

Liam looked up and rubbed his hands together. "Two out of three? My favorite odds!" He laughed loudly, and the pair walked inside the main house to recover from their adventure.

By that time, Bethanie had arrived in the kitchen and was seated at the table, enjoying a glass of fresh orange juice. When she saw the runners, she giggled. "Why are *you* the only one sweating, Alberto?"

Pouring himself into a chair near Bethanie, Alberto laughed and shook his head. "I am afraid your son put me in my place. He's quite an athlete, Bethanie. You didn't tell me!"

Bethanie cocked her head toward Liam and then raised her eyebrows. "I suppose even *I* didn't know that. You must have enjoyed your run today, my little gazelle."

"I have to say, Momma, I had forgotten how fun it is to be outside running." Then his expression softened as he added, "Being with Alberto made it even better."

Bethanie turned her gaze toward Alberto, and a smile crossed her face. "Well, I am glad to hear you both got a good workout. Now how about a bite to eat? I know you're both famished, and I could use the company. I was just waiting on breakfast to come out."

The two runners smiled and nodded their agreement.

They did not have long to wait before a server appeared with a vegetable omelet and fried potatoes for Bethanie. The young man then turned to Alberto and Liam and asked, "What can I get you gentlemen? It looks as if you worked up an appetite."

Alberto gestured to Liam, "What will you have, young athlete?"

Liam grinned. "Pancakes, please."

Alberto cackled. "My thoughts, exactly. We earned it!" With that, he held up two fingers to the server and added, "Two glasses of orange juice also, please."

Liam nodded enthusiastically.

The trio sat and talked while Bethanie enjoyed her omelet. In a few moments, the server returned with two orders of pancakes, complete with small bowls of maple syrup and two large glasses of freshly squeezed orange juice.

"Ah yes, the breakfast of champions," Alberto commented, taking one of the plates and handing it to Liam, then getting his own. The server set down the orange juice, bowed humbly, and walked away.

At one point while the group was enjoying their breakfast, Alberto asked the others, "Would you like me to go with you today to your house? I would be happy to give you a hand."

Bethanie looked at Liam and then replied kindly, "I think we'd like to spend a little time at the house by ourselves today, if you don't mind, Alberto. The drive isn't too long, and it will be nice just to reminisce before we leave for an extended time. We'll pick out the items we would like brought over and then let you know."

"Of course," he agreed. "By the way, we got your car from the lot in Santo Domingo. It's been fueled, and it's ready for you to drive today."

Bethanie crossed her hand over heart. "Thank you, Alberto," she said with a smile.

"It's settled then. I will see you both this evening. I have lots of work to do here today anyway, so we can reconnect at dinner if that's okay."

Bethanie nodded, and the three finished their breakfast and parted ways for the day.

As Liam and Bethanie started down the path to their house, the boy poignantly said, "Thank you, Momma."

She looked back at her son quizzically. "For what?"

Liam grabbed her hand lovingly. "For loving me so much."

Overcome with emotion, she stopped and replied, "Liam . . . I don't know what I have done to deserve you for a son, but I am the luckiest mother in the world."

He reached up and hugged his mother, who said after a minute, "Now I guess we better get going, huh? We've got a busy day today!"

Liam nodded, eased out of the embrace, and then walked on with his mother down the path.

As Bethanie thought about the potential emotions of being back in her home for what could be one of the last times, she inhaled deeply and repeated to herself, *A busy day indeed . . .*

CHAPTER 12

It turned out to be a very busy day, just as the two had expected.

On the way out of town, Bethanie and Liam stopped at a small private school Alberto had referred them to. Even though it was last minute, the administrator was more than happy to meet the Pérezes—especially given their connection to Alberto. The highly rated school was close to the farm, and when a friendly young teacher gave them a tour, both Liam and Bethanie were convinced it was the right place.

"We only have two spots left in Liam's grade, so your timing is excellent," the teacher added. "And since Mr. Rodriguez referred you, Liam is already pre-approved. If you wish to enroll, we'll mail you the paperwork, and you can simply send it back at your convenience."

Bethanie's look of shock prompted the woman to ask if everything was alright.

"This whole process would have taken weeks at Liam's old school, and you just brought it down to an hour! Thank you so much."

The teacher shrugged as the corners of her mouth turned up. "Having Mr. Rodriguez involved makes things happen quite seamlessly around here. He's done so much for so many of us—including the school—we are happy to return the kindness whenever we can." She extended her hand to Bethanie, then turned to Liam and added warmly, "I'll look forward to having you in my class."

Liam beamed, and then the mother and son headed out the door to continue their day of errands.

When they arrived at their little home in Punta Grande, they marked all the items that they wanted to bring to their new place in Santa Guaro, and then took a drive around the neighborhood, reminiscing.

Bethanie pointed out an old playground. "Your dad and I used to take you there every night after supper. We would play with you until you were so tired, you would fall asleep in the swing. Then your dad would pick you up and carry you to the car, and I would carry your stuffed animals—which were always a handful." She smiled.

Liam's face brightened at the memory. "Couldn't forget those, could we?"

As they continued the drive, Bethanie pointed out a few more places steeped in family memories. When they passed a narrow street with small brick houses, Bethanie squinched up her face, searching for a house number. Then she pointed. "There it is, the house your grandmother lived in. After your grandfather died, you were her biggest source of joy. We used to bring you over to her house, and she would fix your favorite cookies every week."

Liam smiled at the thought. "I miss her, Momma. How long has it been?" he asked gently.

"Mother died four years ago, and it seems like just yesterday. I miss her, too. She was so proud of you, Liam. Sometimes I look in your eyes, and I see her . . . " She turned away to keep her son from seeing the tears welling up.

Liam sat quietly as his mom continued "driving down memory lane," as she said. After another hour, she felt fatigue setting in. "Ready to head back home to Alberto's place?"

"I think so, Momma. But it's been a good day here."

When they arrived back at the cocoa farm, they saw a man talking with Alberto in the driveway outside the main house. His skin was golden like that of Liam and his mother, and he had an athletic build under his fitted running suit.

When Liam and Bethanie pulled up and stepped out of their car, the two men walked over to greet them. Alberto waved. "How was your day?"

Bethanie exhaled. "Tiring, but good." Liam nodded his agreement.

Alberto continued, "With everything you needed to do, I can only imagine." Then, gesturing toward the other gentleman, Alberto offered, "Bethanie and Liam, I would like you to meet José Garcia."

Bethanie reached out to shake the gentleman's outstretched hand, but Liam's mouth fell open.

"You mean THE José Garcia?"

He cackled. "Well, I have never been called a THE before, but I guess so."

Liam turned to Alberto in shock. "José is the most famous runner in all the Dominican Republic!" Then, pointing at the visitor, he stuttered, "He, I mean, *you* . . . are a national champion and the coach of the national team!"

The man took off his stylish sunglasses and held up his hands in jest. "Yep, you got me."

Alberto smiled and then spoke up. "I have known José for many years, and we have a wonderful friendship."

José shook his head. "Alberto is modest. The truth is that one of the biggest reasons I became successful was . . . him."

Liam and Bethanie exchanged curious glances as the man continued. "I grew up very poor, and Alberto sponsored me. I was in an orphanage in Puerto Wando, and he happened to come by one day to make a donation. One of the owners had a sports background and suggested to Alberto I might be athletically gifted. Alberto put me in touch with a coach, and I guess the rest is history. I truly believe there is no way I would have become successful without his help."

"You are too kind, José," said Alberto. "However, one thing is for sure—I am grateful I went to the orphanage that day—you put the Dominican Republic on the map, and I now have a friend who has impacted people all over the world."

José nodded humbly and placed his hand over his heart.

Alberto then addressed Liam and his mother. "I wanted José to come by and meet you two. When Ernesto told me he believed Liam had exceptional talent, I was curious. When I saw what happened at sea that day, and then when I saw him run here at the farm . . . I realized this young man, like José, is truly something special. So, I asked my friend to come over and see in person."

Liam's pupils grew wide as he pointed at himself. "Me?"

The men laughed, and José responded, "Yes, *you*. Liam, tomorrow I would like you to come to the track at the school you'll be attending. We can run a bit together. There is no pressure, but I am always interested when I hear about young athletes who have great skill—and a great heart. Alberto says you have both."

Liam took a deep breath and turned to his mother, who glanced at the men, and then her gaze fell to her son. "Liam, would you like to do that?"

The boy's toothy grin was evidence enough of his interest.

José's eyes crinkled. "Okay Liam, how about if I meet you and your mom and Alberto tomorrow morning at the track—say around nine o'clock, after breakfast?"

Liam and Bethanie traded smiles, and the boy replied softly, "Yes, sir. Thank you, Mister Garcia."

"Please, call me José. It was a pleasure meeting you both—and until tomorrow, Liam." The celebrity runner shook each of their hands, then climbed into his car and drove slowly off into the distance.

Liam, Bethanie, and Alberto exchanged looks of happiness, and Alberto asked, "So, what do you think?"

As Liam looked on, the young woman reached out and put her arms around the man in gratitude. "I think," she replied softly, "God has just smiled on our family. Thank you, Alberto . . . ."

CHAPTER 13

After a good night's rest, Liam and Bethanie joined Alberto for breakfast in the main house. After dining on a scrumptious meal of bacon, eggs, and homemade bread and jam, the group was ready to head over to the school to meet José. They climbed into the limousine that Alberto had requested to take them to their meeting with the coach.

On the short drive over, Alberto noted Liam's quietness. "Liam, I want you to remember something. This is simply an opportunity for you to spend some time with a terrific person, doing something that you both love to do—run. Whatever happens, you will have a new friend, and someone who can share with you about running. Just enjoy yourself—and *be* yourself. No pressure."

His face brightened. "'I like that idea."

Bethanie nodded. "I agree. Liam, you will meet many wonderful people in your life, and José is one of those people. His expectations of you are realistic— he is just interested in seeing you run, which you love to do anyway. Plus, I bet you'll find you have a lot in common."

His mother's gentle smile seemed to always make things better, and this was no exception.

He bobbed his head in agreement. "Thank you, Momma."

At that moment, the limousine pulled up to the track where they saw José waiting for them. He smiled and waved at the group as they arrived.

The trio stepped out and walked toward José, then exchanged pleasantries while Liam took in the area, marveling at the beauty of the track.

"Have you seen a track like this before, Liam?" José cocked his head, watching for Liam's response.

"No, sir, but it's . . . beautiful. It reminds me of the track I saw you race on in the national championship."

"Ah, you saw that on TV, did you?"

Liam grinned. "My father and I watched you. I also remember my mom got mad because when you won, we threw our popcorn in the air, and it got all over the living room!" Liam placed his hand over his mouth and snickered.

José chuckled. "Yes, it was quite a day—that race was one I will never forget. Speaking of something that I'll never forget, I would like to see you run. You have already proven to me that you are an unforgettable person, Liam, so we can check that off the list. Let's have some fun on the track, what do you say?" He grinned.

Liam nodded. José gestured toward the open gate leading to the track, and then he pointed to the stands. "Your mom and Alberto can sit in the front row of the bleachers."

With that, Liam and José stepped onto the track and walked a lap together to warm up. As they did, Alberto and Bethanie could see them talking and laughing.

Bethanie turned to Alberto and forced a smile as they sat down. "I'm nervous."

Alberto wrapped his arm around her. "I understand. Me too."

After the lap, José said to the boy, "When I say go, you're off! I want you to run until you get to the marked end of the track—that's one hundred meters. Got it?"

Liam nodded.

"On your mark, get set . . . GO!"

Liam took off. As José watched with wide eyes, the boy crossed the finish line in a blur.

The coach walked down to the end of the track where Liam was now catching his breath. José had not timed him, but he knew he was witnessing the beginning of something extraordinary.

He glanced toward the stands and saw Alberto and Bethanie craning their necks with curious looks on their faces, not knowing whether the boy's speed was unusually good or not. He gave them a thumbs up.

José scratched his head. "Liam, that was . . . very good."

Liam, starting to breathe easier, smiled. The two walked another lap together until they got back to the starting line.

"Could you do that one more time, Liam?"

"Yes, sir, maybe faster," he said with a sly grin.

José tilted his head. "Go right ahead, my friend."

Liam stood in front of the coach, who quietly removed a stopwatch from his pocket.

"On your mark, get set, go!"

José clicked the stopwatch as Liam took off down the track. When the boy crossed the finish line, José clicked the timer once more. His gaze fell to the stopwatch. He raised his sunglasses and looked again as his jaw dropped in disbelief.

José walked to the end of the stretch and stood next to Liam, who had his hands on his hips, breathing heavily.

"How'd I do?" he gasped.

José shook his head. "Why don't we go talk to your mom and Alberto?"

"That bad?" the boy asked nervously.

"Not at all, Liam." They reached the two spectators, and José stood silently in front of them.

Alberto cocked a curious eyebrow. "What's wrong?"

José removed his sunglasses, held the stopwatch up toward Alberto and Bethanie, and then said slowly, "I think this young man is going to be the best one-hundred-meter runner the Dominican Republic has ever seen. . . ."

CHAPTER 14

Alberto turned to Bethanie, stunned looks on their faces, as Bethanie reached down and hugged her son tightly.

"So, I guess that's a good thing?" Liam cracked as the group enthusiastically patted the young boy on the back.

José grinned at Alberto. "How about if I give you and Bethanie a call later so we can talk about this and how we might nurture Liam's skills?"

The pair nodded in unison, took turns shaking the coach's hand, and began their walk back to the waiting limo with Liam.

On the way home, Bethanie asked her son about his time with José.

"He was so nice, Momma. He gave me tips on the one-hundred-meter dash and told me it could be my specialty. Then, as we were walking around the track together, he told me about how he had worked really hard to be the *best*. He said he was grateful to have met Mr. Rodriguez."

Alberto smiled and nodded his appreciation.

Liam then added softly, "Momma, he didn't have a father either when he was growing up."

Seeing his mother's eyes glisten, he pivoted. "Anyway, I feel like José and I have a lot in common." He asked breathlessly, "Do you think he wants to be my coach?"

"Well, let's take things once step at a time, Son, and see where he recommends you start."

The corners of Liam's mouth turned up as he leaned back in the seat—and fell sound asleep.

The next few days were crammed full of activity.

Alberto was tied up with meetings and conference calls, so his presence was scarce to his guests, and Liam and Bethanie were busy arranging the household items that had been delivered from their home in Punta Grande.

In fact, they were all so busy that they almost forgot about the call they were expecting from José . . .

Almost.

When the phone rang, Bethanie pushed her hair back and walked quickly over to pick it up.

"Hello?" Her expression went blank as the caller on the other end began speaking. Liam joined his mother in the kitchen, having heard her pick up the phone.

"Yes, I understand. Yes, okay, okay. Alright, I will tell him—thank you so very much."

Liam scrunched up his face as his mother hung up the phone and turned to him with a shocked look.

"Momma, what is it? Was that Jose'?"

Bethanie suddenly broke into a wide grin. She reached over and hugged her son and cried, "Yes, it was Jose'. Liam, he said your time is already the best in the Dominican Republic for your age!"

"It *is*?"

"Yes! He said he believes you're going to be a champion. Liam," she stuttered, "he wants to be your coach, and he said Alberto has generously agreed to take care of the fees. He also says you've got a real shot at getting more sponsors later on!"

The boy jumped up excitedly, but then quickly added, "But, Momma, where will I go? I won't have to move, will I? Momma, I can't leave you. . . ."

Bethanie shook her head and offered a reassuring smile. "He said he will work with you after school, and in the mornings if necessary. Jose' works here with other athletes too, and you will be able to meet them and practice together."

Bethanie hesitated and then added, "So . . . what do you think?"

Liam looked out the big bay window at the sprawling fields, and then turned back to his mother. "I think Father would be proud."

With that, Bethanie swept the boy off his feet, shut her eyes, and embraced him tightly. "Yes, he would, Liam—he definitely would."

"When do we start, Momma?"

His mother pushed his hair out of his eyes. "School starts in three days, and he said he would meet you at the track after class."

Liam nodded, and the pair went back to work arranging their home. But the conversation the rest of the day was on a totally different subject. . . .

CHAPTER 15

That night at dinner with Alberto, Bethanie and Liam excitedly detailed the conversation with Jose'—and expressed their deep gratitude.

Hearing this, the man smiled broadly. "José has coached many champion athletes, and there are hundreds of runners who would love to work with him. He's the national coach, and the fact that he has chosen Liam speaks for itself."

Bethanie looked over at her son and raised an eyebrow. "It will be a lot of work."

Alberto added, "A new school, a new home, a new sport, a new coach. That's a lot of fresh starts, Liam. Are you sure you don't want to wait until you're settled in at your new school?"

Liam shook his head. "I'm ready."

Alberto and Bethanie nodded and smiled at each other. The trio enjoyed their meal and then headed into the den for more spirited conversation about the adventure that lay ahead for Liam.

The end of the summer break came quickly, and when the first day of school arrived, Liam and Bethanie took the trip together by foot. It was only half a mile away, plus it was a pleasant walk through the countryside, and the weather was warm.

"Now, remember," Bethanie reminded him, "always be on your best behavior, and be respectful of the teachers."

Liam shook his head. "Momma, you know you taught me well."

Bethanie grinned.

A few minutes later, the pair reached the small school building. The same young teacher they had met before walked up to them. "Hi, Liam, welcome back! Ready for your first day?"

Liam nodded and offered a nervous smile. "Yes, ma'am."

"Good. We finish at three o'clock, and then I will walk you over to the track to meet Coach José."

Bethanie offered her appreciation before adding to Liam, "See you soon, Son. I will meet you at the track."

Liam waved goodbye, and the teacher ushered him into the classroom. "Everyone, this is Liam."

The ten students flashed their smiles at him. "Hi, Liam!" they returned.

For the first time in a long time, Liam Pérez felt like he belonged.

The day was full of "firsts" for Liam, and once the final bell rang, the students packed up their schoolbooks and headed off in different directions. "Let's go this way," Liam's teacher said. "It's a shortcut to the track."

Liam nodded, feeling slightly nervous at what lay ahead, and the two headed down a path to where the practices would be held.

When they arrived, Coach José was there to greet them with a broad smile on his face. "Well, well, if it isn't my new track star—and one of my favorite teachers!" He winked playfully at the blushing woman.

Liam's attention was drawn away to his mother, who came running over to join them. "How was the day?" she asked breathlessly.

"It was a great day, Momma. But . . . I've been looking forward to my coaching all day, too!"

Hearing that, José chuckled. "And it's just you and me today, Liam. This will give us a chance to get to know each other a little bit, and next time, we will have the whole group with us."

Liam bunched his eyebrows. "The whole group?"

"Yes, there are around a dozen athletes training with me at any given time. Many are on the Dominican national team, and some are training for the Olympics or the World Championships—and a few are new, like you. They're older than you, but your time will come."

The boy nodded and smiled his approval.

José and Liam walked out to the track and began going through some warm-up exercises, each of which the coach would carefully explain and demonstrate. "Always start with a little stretching, you know? Don't want to pull a muscle."

Liam was focusing hard on the coach's gestures and instructions.

"That's right, Liam—just a little more to the left," he added as Liam reached his arm across his shoulder. "You're actually very flexible—that's good!"

Bethanie watched nervously from the stands, but she was happy to see her son smiling and engaged.

Then she saw the coach gesture to Liam, and the boy moved toward the starting line. A whistle blew, and Liam sprinted. He ran full-out for one hundred meters, and then he thrust his fists in the air at the finish line. The coach was just a few yards behind him.

"Great, just like that! Raise those arms into the air like the champion you are!" José called out.

Liam was grinning ear to ear as the coach joined him to walk slowly around the track.

"Once more, Liam."

The boy nodded, and the coach moved back into position as Liam set up at the start line. The whistle blew again, and Liam tore ahead once more, arms pumping. This time, he appeared to run even faster.

At one hundred meters, José checked his stopwatch and shook his head. "That's impressive, Liam. Let's go once more." Without hesitation, the young runner grinned back at him and got into position again.

The practice and instruction continued for another hour. When they finished, the two walked over to Bethanie who was reading in the front row of the bleachers. As they approached, she closed her book, looked up, and smiled. "I was exhausted just watching you two," she said, exhaling loudly. "Wow!"

José chuckled. "Well, this is the life of an athlete—and I must say, he did great on his first day."

The boy flashed a wide grin at his mother.

"Tomorrow, most of the athletes I coach will practice together here. Liam will get a chance to meet them all. He's going to fit in just fine."

Relief crossed Bethanie's face as José looked at his watch and added, "Gotta run—I'll see you both tomorrow at the same time." With that, the coach jogged over to his vehicle, jumped in, and slowly pulled out of sight.

Bethanie shook her head. "It's a lot of work, Son. But I know you can do it."

He smiled. "Me, too. Coach José told me today about the challenges he faced when he was my age. He told me how lucky I am to have a mother because he did not have either of his parents."

A compassionate frown appeared on the young woman's face. "We all have our crosses to bear, don't we, Liam?"

He agreed with a nod.

"Let's walk home," Bethanie suggested, "and we can talk a little more about your day."

The two Pérezes turned down the path back to their house and chatted excitedly the whole way. Arriving back at the farm, they stepped inside their home, and Liam plopped down on a couch in the living room. Bethanie grabbed a cool glass of water and brought it to her son as she sat down beside him.

Handing him the drink, she gently pushed his hair back out of his eyes. "Why don't we rest for a few minutes, and then we will go to dinner at the main house. Alberto won't be here tonight—he has a dinner meeting—but we can enjoy a nice meal before we turn in early. You could use some extra rest after your first day."

Liam nodded in agreement, and the weary pair closed their eyes. Before they realized it, they were sound asleep until the grandfather clock chimed six an hour later.

Bethanie jumped up. "I guess we needed that rest, Son, but we should hurry if we want to be on time for dinner!"

Liam nodded as he sat up and rubbed his eyes. After washing up and changing clothes, they were seated in the dining room in under fifteen minutes.

"Did you make any new friends at school today?" Bethanie asked with interest as they enjoyed their *soncocho*, a tasty Dominican stew made with plantains, beef, chicken, pork, and a variety of fresh vegetables.

Liam smiled. "Not yet, but everyone seemed nice. They also loved that I am running track."

Bethanie grinned. "My son, the super athlete."

Liam shook his head. "Not yet, but someday . . ."

"I do like the fact that your class is small," Bethanie commented. "The school in Punta Grande was so full that you didn't even have a desk some days. I just can't believe you are in a private school . . . I would have loved to go to a school like yours when I was younger." Bethanie sighed. "But, I'm so happy that *you* do."

Liam looked affectionately at his mother. Soon they were both full—and getting sleepy again. "Well, let's head back, and we can look over some of your schoolbooks."

They were back at the house in just a few minutes, and after a little more talk about the school day, Bethanie saw Liam's fatigue setting in quickly. Watching her son nearly fall asleep mid-conversation, she stood him up and helped him into bed.

Bethanie covered him and walked quietly to the door to turn off the light, then glanced back at her son and whispered softly, "Goodnight, my gentle warrior. . . ." as she pulled his door shut.

CHAPTER 16

Liam's mother walked him to school again the next day, and when they arrived, he was greeted again by the petite, enthusiastic young teacher.

"Are you ready for another good day?"

Liam nodded. "Yes, ma'am!"

His mother gave the boy a quick kiss on the top of his head, and then turned and headed back to the farm as Liam jogged into the classroom. All the children waved at him as some also said hello, and his sense of belonging was increasing daily.

At recess, a little girl with sparkling brown eyes and a bouncing black ponytail wandered over to Liam. "I'm Maria," she said with a disarming smile. "You're the new boy who's so good in track, aren't you?"

Liam blushed. "Um, I guess so. Thank you."

"Can I come and watch you run sometime? I hear you could be the next great Dominican runner." She raised her eyebrows and added in a soft voice, "That way, I can tell my friends I know someone famous!"

Liam dragged his shoe across the ground and replied, "Well, I'm not great yet, but I will be someday." He cut his eyes in anticipation of her next comment, but instead, the girl smiled, turned, and skipped away. She glanced back after a few yards and said with a grin, "Bye, track star."

Liam laughed under his breath as he realized . . . he liked Maria—for a girl.

When Liam arrived at track practice that afternoon, he was nervous, wondering who all would be there. Was he going to be the only new kid? Was he going to be the slowest? Was he even good enough to be here?

His thoughts were interrupted by the baritone voice of José. "Come on, slowpoke!" Liam saw the coach and six other runners standing on the track near the entrance. They were getting warmed up for their practice, stretching and jogging in place.

"Alright, everybody, listen up! I would like to introduce you to our youngest team member, Liam Pérez!" The coach clapped as Liam walked toward the group.

Any worry Liam had of not being accepted was gone now as the entire team clapped and yelled his name.

A broad smile crossed his face as each team member patted him on the back and rubbed his head—as if he was already a hero.

After a few moments of Coach José introducing the team, he gestured for the athletes to start their slow warm-up jogs around the track.

"Liam, stay here for just a moment. You can catch up with them in a second."

The youth took a deep breath, which the coach did not miss. "Not to worry, Liam. Nothing's wrong. I just want to share something with you."

As he came closer, José reached out and put his hands on the boy's shoulders. "Liam, these folks will become like family to you. You saw their enthusiasm when you walked over—that was genuine."

Liam's eyes sparkled.

"You are here with the best of the best in Dominican Republic. Each of you has been chosen because of your unique skill—and you must stay together. Do you understand?"

Liam replied softly, "Yes, thank you, Coach José."

José nodded. "Good, now get out there and catch up with your team."

Liam took off after the group, which was about to finish their first lap. After two more rounds, a tall Dominican boy of about sixteen motioned behind himself to the group. "Okay, that's it for warm-up." Liam noticed the other athletes follow his lead.

A boy of about fourteen leaned over. "Jorge is our team captain. He knows everything we are supposed to do—he is kind of like Coach José's assistant."

"Ah, gotcha," Liam said with an understanding nod. "Thanks."

Before Liam could ask the boy his name, José walked out to the track where the team was now standing in a circle. He gave directions for each athlete to follow, and the team prepared to fan out to every part of the track—sprinting, jumping, lifting, whatever event they were training for.

"We all have our specialties," José explained to Liam in front of the group. "As I told you before, we are going to start training you in the hundred-meter dash—I've seen you do it enough to know that you certainly have potential there!" The team clapped and whistled.

"Sounds good, Coach. Thank you."

With that, the squad spread apart. The coach stayed with Liam and began working on improving the boy's technique, then José moved around the track to assist every athlete in their forte.

After an hour and a half, the team was exhausted, and José called the athletes over to the stadium entrance. Even though most were catching their breath, they were still patting each other on the back, shaking hands, and laughing. Liam felt so good being part of a group—it was exactly what he needed.

The coach gave a final word of encouragement, and all the athletes circled up, put their hands on top of each other's hands in a parting show of unity, and cheered, "Go, Dominican Republic!" Then José blew the whistle, and the team dispersed.

Bethanie arrived to see her son walking off the track toward her. She smiled, reached out her arms, and hugged the boy as he came close.

"Ah, it looks like someone had another great day," she said with a wink.

"It was GREAT! Momma, they like me!"

"Well, of course they do—what's not to like?" She laughed. "Come on, let's go home and get something to eat—I know you're hungry."

As they began their short journey home, Liam couldn't stop talking. "Momma, you should see some of these kids run! And jump! They're incredible."

"You are fortunate to be around such high achievers. I don't know how we got so blessed to have all these wonderful things happening to us, but I don't take them for granted."

Liam nodded, and his mother followed up with a question. "So, how was your friend Maria today?" She offered a sly, knowing smile.

Without asking how she knew about the girl, he proudly replied, "I think she might be my best friend soon, Momma. She reminds me of . . ."

"Yes?" Bethanie raised a curious eyebrow.

"Well, she reminds me of you."

Bethanie's eyes crinkled. "How's that?"

"She doesn't say a bad word about anyone. Plus, she is always making sure other people are not left out of things . . . the same way you do."

Bethanie put a loving arm around her son as they continued to walk. "Thank you, my wonderful young man." She leaned over and kissed him on the head. "We will have to get Maria to come visit us at the house sometime."

"I'd like that," Liam grinned. "But, how did you know about her?"

Bethanie tapped her temple. "Mothers know everything—just remember that." She laughed and rubbed Liam's shoulders as he playfully rolled his eyes.

A few minutes later, they were home on the farm. "I hope Alberto is back in town," Bethanie mused. "You've got to catch him up on your first days of school and track."

Liam agreed. He had already worked up an appetite, so he headed back to his room to get ready for dinner. About half an hour later, he was showered and changed.

"Ready?" Bethanie asked, waiting by the front door.

Before Liam could answer, there came a knock. Bethanie opened the door to see who it was.

"Eliza! How are you?"

"I'm doing just fine, but I haven't heard from either of you in a couple of days, so I just wanted to make sure you were alright."

Bethanie smiled. "Yes, we are, thank you. But how about we all walk together over to the main dining room—for old times' sake?" She laughed, and Eliza heartily agreed.

"Of course, right this way," she offered a sweeping gesture to the outside, then followed behind them, closing the large, heavy door.

On the short walk over to the main house, Eliza called ahead to Liam. "So, how is school going, Liam?"

"Very good. I think I'm getting smarter already!"

The boy laughed, and his mother shook her head. "He's definitely learning a lot," she replied. "He's even made some friends—including a girl."

Liam turned to his mother and grinned sheepishly. "Momma . . ."

They reached the main house, and Thomas opened the door as if he knew the three were there.

"Welcome, Pérez family!" He gestured for them to enter, which they did.

Eliza added, "I think I'll head back to the house— you're in good hands now." Then she said in a barely audible voice, "You'll have to tell me about your new friend sometime. I'm sure she's very nice." She winked at Liam.

The pair waved goodbye and thanked her, then began walking into the home, and as they entered, they saw Alberto sitting at the dinner table. He stood and smiled, though his fatigue was evident. As Bethanie and Liam approached, he embraced each of them warmly.

"I'm glad to see you back in town, Alberto, but . . . you look exhausted," she said compassionately.

The man sat down slowly and replied, "It was a long trip, and there were plenty of people who made for a difficult few days, so it's nice to be home." Then he added in a more cheerful tone, "Now, I want to hear all about our scholar athlete!"

Liam nodded shyly, but then spoke in an excited tone. "Alberto, I can't believe this has all worked out for us—thank you so much. Each day seems to be better than the one before."

Alberto applauded. "Tell me more!"

"I am learning so much in school, and I love my teacher. I have made friends—and speaking of friends, I have a whole team of them who Coach José says are the best of the best in the Dominican Republic. How lucky am I to be training with them?"

Just then, a server brought out three steaming plates piled high with spaghetti and meat sauce. Liam's eyes widened. "I love spaghetti!"

"The bolognese here is the finest in the Dominican Republic," Alberto said with pride, "so eat up!"

Liam began digging into the meal, and the rest of the evening was spent in lively, engaging conversation. When everyone had finished eating, Alberto turned to Bethanie. "May we speak on the porch?"

She looked surprised, but quickly agreed. "Yes, of course. Liam, please go to your room and get started on your homework, okay?"

Liam nodded and expressed his gratitude for the dinner before heading back home. Alberto and Bethanie stood and made their way out on the balcony.

Just then, another server brought them two glasses of red wine, which they each took with thanks as the worker went back inside.

"Is everything alright, Alberto?" Bethanie's worry was quickly noted by Alberto, who pivoted to gaze out over the balcony.

After a few seconds, he turned back and said quietly, "Better than alright." Then the corners of his lips turned up.

She raised an eyebrow and cocked her head as he continued.

"I talked with José' earlier today."

Bethanie nodded tentatively and began to smile as he continued. "He thinks Liam might be one of the most talented students he has ever coached."

"Really?"

"Yes, and . . . he also said that he has already gotten everything approved to bring Liam to full sponsorship with the Dominican Republic Track and Field Association. That means they will cover *everything* he needs for the sport. They believe that in five years, he will be competing in national and international events. All his training and travel will be provided for, and they will even pay for a tutor when he is on the road."

"On the road?" Bethanie was shocked. "Like . . . to where? Alberto, he has only just reached his twelfth birthday!"

Alberto shrugged and then said reassuringly, "His travel will increase gradually over the years. Of course, the association would cover all *your* costs also."

Bethanie shook her head and then palmed the back of her neck. "This is so incredible—and it's all happening so fast."

"Yes, I agree. However, I think Ernesto saw this coming—he seemed to know this was Liam's destiny."

Bethanie exhaled loudly. "I know it's an incredible opportunity." She paused and then added, "I will tell Liam tonight."

"Very good." Alberto slowly leaned over to touch Bethanie's soft cheek and continued to reassure her. "I know this is a lot to take in." He then pulled back from the compassionate gaze into her eyes and gently shook his head. "Who would have thought . . . from a small town to the global spotlight? What an amazing journey this will be."

Bethanie nodded. At that moment, she realized that soon her son would not just belong to her . . . he would belong to the world.

CHAPTER 17

That evening, Bethanie talked with her overjoyed son. "Momma, we'll never get another chance like this again. And . . . I know Father has a guiding hand in this somehow." The boy smiled as his mother reached out and hugged him tenderly.

When she pulled away, Bethanie looked into Liam's wide eyes. "Well, son, tomorrow I will talk to the coach and find out more."

Liam nodded, and his mom gave him a kiss on the forehead before they both turned in for the night.

The next day, Liam struggled to focus on his schoolwork. The track journey that lay ahead was all he could think about.

Aside from Maria, that is.

He wanted to tell her so badly about the great news, but he knew he should wait.

The two were fast becoming special friends, and he even decided to give her a ring to show how much she meant to him. His mother had found one in a small thrift shop, and when she brought it home, Liam was ecstatic. The gold band and the bright green stone were certainly going to be a surprise—and when he gave Maria the gift one morning before school, it *was* a hit. She covered her mouth and squealed in delight as her face lit up.

"Thank you, Liam. I will *always* be your girlfriend— no one will be able to separate us." She hugged the boy tightly, kissed him on the cheek, and then turned and skipped away, leaving Liam speechless.

His lips parted and his face flushed as he gently touched the freshly-kissed cheek.

After that, time could not go by quickly enough. Now that he had given Maria the ring, the only thing that could make his day better would be getting the sponsorship news directly from Coach José.

When the bell finally rang at the end of the day, Liam jumped up, told Maria and his classmates goodbye, and sprinted down to the track. When he got there, Bethanie and José were already in deep conversation. José saw Liam out of the corner of his eye, and he waved the boy over.

"Hi, Coach José. Hi Momma," Liam offered with a broad grin.

"Hey, Liam! I was just talking through some of the details with your mom. I know Alberto told you both about the offer."

Liam glanced at his mom, and they both nodded.

"So, Liam will be training with and learning from the best coaches and athletes in the Dominican Republic, and in a few years, he will start competing in major events. Every necessary expense will be covered. Does that sound good?" The man glanced at Bethanie, and then raised an eyebrow in curiosity at Liam.

"Yes, sir!"

José rubbed his hands together. "Great! I'll continue to give you both more details as I learn more. The Association will be excited to have this young athlete on board."

He smiled at Liam. "Okay, my friend, grab your workout clothes and get changed—time to work!" The coach reached out and rubbed the boy's head playfully before Liam took off for the locker room.

Bethanie stayed and exchanged a few more words with the coach before asking her only burning question. "Do you think this is the right decision, José? I mean . . . he is so young."

He nodded. "I understand how you feel, Mrs. Pérez. We will take good care of Liam, and you and Alberto will be kept informed about everything." He hesitated and then added, "To answer your question, yes, this is the right decision—we need to start his training early. Liam . . . is going to impact the world."

Hearing those words, Bethanie smiled, turned away, and quietly took her seat for the day's practice.

FIVE YEARS LATER

As the months and years went by, Liam became stronger, faster, and more skilled. At every practice, he soaked up the coach's words and worked tirelessly to implement the lessons into his form.

Word slowly spread through the Caribbean running community about "the super athlete" down in the Dominican Republic.

At practice, Liam's teammates were astounded at his near world-class speed. He dominated local and regional events that Coach José periodically entered him in "just to see" how Liam was progressing.

During those years, the squad of athletes continued to take Liam under their wings, as if he were a little brother. When they traveled to other cities for national and international meets, he was increasingly present with his teammates. Though he couldn't participate yet, it gave Liam opportunities to study the great runners—always waiting for Coach José to give him the green light to compete.

"Soon, you'll be running these races with us, Liam—and the world better be ready," his teammates would say. Liam would smile . . . waiting eagerly for those days to come.

As his eighteenth birthday approached, José felt it was almost time.

Meanwhile, Maria continued to fulfill her childhood promise of always being there for Liam. At every practice, Maria was beside Bethanie . . . watching and cheering for the astounding progress the young man was making.

At school, the two were inseparable. Then one day, as they sat at their usual lunch table with friends, a teacher approached and whispered in Liam's ear. Terror overtook his face.

"Liam, what is it?" Maria begged.

"My mother. She fell near the creek at the farm and hit her head. One of the workers found her lying on the rocks. I have to go—she's at the hospital."

Sadness clouded the girl's features. "I'm going with you."

Dashing out the door, they were met by a driver and a limousine. "Alberto sent me to get you, Liam—we'll take you both, let's go." The man helped Maria into the back seat of the limousine, and Liam slid in beside her.

"Hurry, please," Liam urged the man. "Do you know anything about my mom's condition?"

The driver pursed his lips and shook his head. "All I know is that a supervisor found her lying by the creek—she had apparently slipped on the rocks. When the ambulance got there, she was in and out of consciousness." The man paused. "She was asking for you, Liam."

Liam put his head in his hands and wept as Maria reached over and squeezed his shoulder tightly.

When they finally got to the hospital, Liam jumped out with Maria and dashed inside to the front desk. "We're here to see Bethanie Pérez."

The nurse, a kind woman in her thirties, flipped through her papers. "She's in Room 236. You're her son?"

"Yes," he replied quickly, and before the receptionist could ask about his companion, Liam blurted out, "this is my wife."

Maria shot Liam a surprised glance, and the receptionist raised an eyebrow but did not press any further. She pointed past the desk. "The doctor is with her now. Down the hallway and around the corner, you'll find her room."

They walked briskly down the corridor and reached Bethanie's room just as a middle-aged man in a white coat stepped out. "You must be Liam," he said neutrally.

Liam fired back in a panicked voice. "Yes, can I see her?"

The doctor nodded. "She has not lost consciousness since she's been here. Hopefully we will not have to operate—and she can just rest and recover, but we will know more in the next few hours when her tests come back," he said. "She has a serious concussion, and she lost a lot of blood from the wound. I would say they got her here just in time—otherwise she would be in intensive care now."

Liam breathed a sigh of relief, as did Maria. The doctor gently pushed the door open wider and gestured inside before following them.

As the trio approached the bed, Bethanie's eyes widened, although her voice was weak. "Liam, Maria, you came. I am so happy to see you both."

Liam grabbed his mother's soft hands. "Of course we did, Momma. As soon as we heard what happened, we were on our way."

"But, your school . . . and your running," she protested.

Liam put a finger to her lips. "It will all still be there."

Bethanie smiled as Liam bent down and kissed her on the forehead while Maria tenderly pulled the covers up around the woman.

"Guess I needed my rock-throwing champion with me. I could have used you there to keep me out of trouble, Liam." She winked.

He shook his head and pointed at her playfully. "If your wish this time had anything to do with being in a hospital, it came true fast."

She rubbed her temples and closed her eyes. "I'm not exactly sure what happened—my memory is a little fuzzy, but I do know that I had just gone for a walk—down to where we usually go together."

Liam nodded. "Don't worry about it now, Momma. What you need to do is rest. I am going to stay here the rest of the day, and longer if needed."

Right then, Alberto burst through the door. "Bethanie! What happened? I was out of town when I got the call, and I got here as quickly as I could . . ." Seeing Liam and Maria, he asked, "Is she alright?" Then he turned back to Bethanie. "*Are* you?"

She reached out to squeeze Alberto's hand. "I'll be fine. Just a little bump on the head," she added with a soft laugh. "It seems Liam is the great runner of the family, and I'm not even a good walker!" She forced a smile but then felt a stab of pain, and she winced.

The three immediately lunged forward to help, but then Bethanie closed her eyes and waved her hand dismissively. "Don't fuss over me. The doctors said the pain will come and go for a while."

Alberto squeezed her hand with concern, his face pale. "Bethanie, I was terrified when I heard you had been hurt. I have gotten so used to having you and Liam with me . . . you are my family now." Tears now rolled down the man's ruddy cheeks as he reached out and hugged all three of them.

Liam looked first at Maria, then turned his gaze to his mother. Bethanie smiled as she savored the embrace of the group.

The doctor stepped forward and said pointedly, "Let's give her something to help her rest now."

The three nodded in unison as the doctor ushered them gently out the door and closed it behind them.

Liam and Maria stayed in the waiting room for the next few hours with Alberto. As evening approached, Alberto suggested, "Liam, why don't you two go to the farm and get some dinner. I'll stay here with your mom until you get back, and I'll let you know immediately if there is any news."

Before Liam could respond, Maria answered, "Great idea. To best take care of her, we must take care of ourselves also." She reached out to touch her boyfriend's cheek tenderly.

"You're right." Liam turned to Alberto. "Let us know if we can bring you anything. We'll be back soon."

Alberto nodded in appreciation, and the pair quietly slipped out the door where they rejoined the limo and headed to the farm.

No matter how many times she had been to the property, Maria was always amazed at the beauty of the land and the homeplace, and when they stepped inside the main house, she marveled at the dining room. "Do you ever pinch yourself?" she stammered.

"Often." Liam grinned.

"I would, too!"

Right then, a server came over and brought several trays of food: hamburgers, French fries, a variety of sandwiches . . . it was a feast.

As they enjoyed their dinner, Liam's thoughts were never far from his mother. "She just . . ." His sentence was interrupted by the phone ringing. One of the staff members answered the call, and then quickly handed the phone to Liam.

"Yes?"

He heard the voice of Coach José on the other line, inquiring about Bethanie.

"Thank goodness they think she will be okay," he breathed as Liam related to him the status of his mother.

"Liam," the coach continued, "I want you to think about something . . ."

Liam listened intently. "I was going to tell you this at practice today. Due to an unexpected disqualification, there is an opening for us to compete in the All-Caribbean meet in Puerto Rico at the end of next week. I want you to represent us in the one-hundred-meter dash."

Liam's face went pale. "Me? Coach, do you . . . I mean, do we . . . think I'm ready?"

"You are."

The young man stuttered, "I . . . I can't leave my mother. She needs me here."

There was a lengthy pause, and then the coach gently added, "Liam, you'll have to make that choice, and I will understand either way. But if it sounds like she is going to be fine—especially after another week of healing—you should strongly consider it. She has the best doctors in the Dominican Republic at that hospital. Talk it over with your mom tomorrow, and you can let me know. There's no rush—I just need to have an answer in a couple of days."

Liam slowly nodded. "Okay, Coach, I'll let you know as soon as possible."

Liam hung up the phone and stared blankly at Maria.

"What was that about, Liam?"

"He wants me to compete in the All-Caribbean meet with the team. In Puerto Rico."

Her eyes were like saucers. "Liam, this is what you've been waiting for! I'm so proud of you!"

He shrugged. "Thank you, but . . . my mother. I can't . . ."

She interrupted, sensing his struggle. "You're right—it's a tough call." Then she added, "If it seems your mom is doing better, and you want to say yes to the track meet, Alberto and I will look after Bethanie. You won't be gone more than a few days, right?"

He nodded slowly.

"Listen," Maria hastened to add, "we'll talk to your mom, and I have a feeling she will say the same thing. She'll insist you go."

Liam and Maria finished their dinner, and after about a half hour, the young man suggested, "Let's go back to the hospital for a little while, and then we need to get you home."

As they stood to leave, Liam embraced the girl. "Thank you," he said softly.

Maria smiled, reached for the young man's hand, then kissed it tenderly. . . .

CHAPTER 18

Once again, a car from Alberto was waiting as the two stepped outside the house, and soon they were back at the hospital.

When they walked into her room, Bethanie was sitting up in bed, and Alberto stood beside her, stroking her forehead tenderly. "She slept like a baby while you two were gone. They want to keep her for a few more days as a precaution, but her test results came back negative. I think she's going to be back to her old self soon," he said with a big grin.

Liam walked over and spoke gently to his mother. "You can't scare us like that anymore, Momma. We need you." He picked up her hand and held it against his cheek.

"I will always be there for you, Liam the Great." She smiled broadly.

"Momma, I haven't heard you use that nickname in years."

He shook his head and laughed as Maria added, "I don't think I have ever heard him called that." Her eyes sparkled. "It's got a nice ring to it—but don't get *too* used to it from me." She playfully pointed her finger at Liam.

He grinned, but then his expression became blank. "Momma, Coach José called me earlier."

His mother raised a curious eyebrow as Liam continued. "He wants me to compete in my first major race."

Bethanie clasped her hands together. "That's wonderful news!"

Alberto chimed in, "Liam, this is your dream! Congratulations!"

Liam glanced sheepishly over at Maria, who cocked an eyebrow at him. He then looked back at his mother. "Momma, it's next week . . . in Puerto Rico. I told him you are my priority."

A hush fell over the room, then Bethanie motioned for her son to come closer. She cupped his face softly with both hands and spoke. "Liam Pérez, this is your time to shine. I'll be fine. If I need you, I will know how to find you, but you must go—it is your destiny, Liam. Remember?"

Liam smiled and then pulled away slowly from his mother. "Momma, if this is what you believe and what you want me to do, I'll follow your wishes."

"Yes, Liam, of course it's what I want. The doctor said I would be released in a few days, and while you're gone, I will give Alberto strict instructions to keep me away from the creek until my stone-skipping partner returns."

The corners of the young man's mouth turned up. "Okay, Momma. I will let José know tomorrow."

"We'll take good care of her," came Alberto's voice. "Even though she can't be at the meet, we will make sure we have a TV all set up so our patient can watch you on the big day." He smiled at Bethanie.

The four talked some more until the nurse entered the room. "Visiting hours are over, I am afraid. You can come back tomorrow morning." She gestured to the door, and the group slowly filed out, each wishing Bethanie goodnight as they left.

Alberto turned to Maria and offered, "You're of course welcome to stay with us, or we can have someone drop you off at your house."

She thanked him and then shook her head. "I'd like to spend a little time with my parents tonight, so if you would take me home, that would be great."

Alberto nodded, and the three headed downstairs to the waiting car.

The next morning, Alberto was up and out of the house quickly to attend early meetings while Liam slept in a little later before heading to school.

Alberto stopped by the hospital to check on Bethanie, and to his pleasant surprise, when he stepped into her room, she was awake and seemed alert—which the attending nurse validated. The three of them talked for a few minutes, and when he left for his meetings, Alberto contacted Liam to reassure him that his mother was doing fine. The young man was ecstatic to hear the report.

All the students had heard about Liam's mother, so when he got to school that morning, they each expressed their sadness at her fall, but also their relief that she was going to be alright.

Then one of the girls asked, "Liam, is it true you are going to run in the All-Caribbean meet?"

The room was suddenly filled with chatter and excitement. "Really, Liam, is that true?"

Maria sat at a desk nearby, carefully guarding her expression as Liam laughed nervously. "Wow, word travels fast around here, huh? I haven't even told my coach yet."

As though on cue, José walked in the door. The teacher pointed to Liam and said with a grin, "Coach José said he wanted to speak directly with you this morning to get your answer, instead of the hearsay that's going around, so I told him to stop by and let Liam share the news with the class, too." She smiled slyly.

José turned to Liam. "Well, Liam, I'm with your classmates—I'd like to know." He grinned, and a hush fell over the students.

Liam glanced around the room at his long-time friends. In an instant, his thoughts went back to the devastated young boy who had lost his father. He remembered how this very group had helped soothe his early, painful feelings of alienation and aloneness.

Liam cut his eyes toward a now nodding Maria, then turning back toward his coach, he said resolutely, "Yes, sir, Coach . . . I'm in."

The room erupted. Chants of LIAM, LIAM, LIAM filled the air as the coach walked over and shook Liam's hand. He quietly added with a smile, "See you at practice today, Champ," then turned and walked out the door.

Liam looked at his friends, who were now standing, patting him on the back and rubbing his head playfully.

"You all know how to make a guy feel good," he said with a broad smile.

"Yeah, and no pressure—you just better win," one of the students said with a laugh.

That afternoon, and for the next few days before the team's departure for Puerto Rico, Liam went to practice as usual, but with more commitment and determination than ever. He visualized the stadium, the track, and the other runners. During the workouts, he imagined himself competing against other great athletes from across the Caribbean—and "saw" himself crossing the finish line in first place.

As if Coach José could read Liam's mind, he constantly reminded Liam during practice, "*See* victory, Liam. See yourself pushing in a way that you never have. See yourself relaxed, strong, confident—and visualize your win."

The other teammates were busy preparing for their own events. They were all incredibly focused and excited about the opportunity to compete at the All-Caribbean meet. But even as single-minded as the athletes were, they still found time during practice to reach out to their "younger brother" and encourage him for his first big race. "You got this, Liam!" echoed through the workout sessions.

Every day at the end of practice, Liam was more excited than ever about the upcoming race, indeed more than anything he could remember participating in. José had reminded the young man that he was prepared—very well prepared.

Liam's daily routine was school, track practice, hospital. He told his mother, who was improving daily, everything about his intense practice sessions. Then it was back to the farm for dinner with Alberto and homework. Then, the two would go back to the hospital until visiting hours were over.

At the conclusion of the last practice before the team would leave for the meet, Liam said confidently, "This is going to be a race I'll never forget, Coach."

José reached over and put his hand on the runner's shoulder. "I have no doubt about that. You've been training for this since you were eleven years old. Now, let's finish off this practice so everyone can go home and start packing. We only have two more days until our flight for Puerto Rico."

With that, he blew his whistle, and the group circled up for a few final inspiring words before going home.

That evening, Liam, Alberto, and Maria helped bring Bethanie home from the hospital, and once they arrived back at the farm, the house staff was waiting out in front of their home to greet them. Bethania stepped slowly out of the car toward the group, gazed around the property, and said with a sigh, "Oh, how I have missed this place."

Eliza quickly moved forward to gently assist the woman. "We all missed you, too. It's not the same around here when you're gone, Mrs. Pérez." She smiled.

Bethanie nodded, and the welcoming party joined in to carefully help her into the house.

"Momma," Liam gestured toward the recliner in her room, "let's put you over here right now. You can watch TV and hopefully a network will carry the meet in Puerto Rico."

Settling into the comfortable chair, she asked, "Speaking of Puerto Rico, are you ready, Son?"

Liam nodded and said resolutely, "Coach said I couldn't be any more ready. I'm excited."

Just then, his smile slipped, and he added, "I just wish the three of you could come too."

"We will be there in spirit, my son. Trust me." She gently reached out and held Liam's hand.

Alberto glanced up at the clock. "It's almost dinnertime. Would you like us to bring something back to the room for you?"

Bethanie shook her head. "Thank you, but I am not hungry yet. You three go ahead and eat." She looked at Maria and added, "Don't let these boys stuff themselves too much."

Maria laughed. "I'll keep an eye on them."

The group waved goodbye as they headed to the main house for a meal and some more conversation about the upcoming competition. After dinner, Liam and Maria returned to the house where they found Bethanie asleep in the recliner, the bandage on her head still attached securely. Liam glanced at the covered wound and shook his head.

"I know what you're thinking. It could have been much worse, right?" Maria put her hands affectionately on Liam's shoulders.

"Yes," Liam agreed. "So much worse." Then he glanced at his watch. "Ah, your parents will be wondering where you are—we need to get you home!" He escorted her to the front of the main house and then stepped inside and spoke with Alberto, who immediately summoned a driver to take the girl home.

Liam then stepped back out to the front, and when the chauffeur arrived, the gentleman opened the car door for Maria. She stepped toward her boyfriend, then kissed her finger and touched it to Liam's lips softly. "Pleasant dreams. See you tomorrow at school."

He embraced the girl lovingly, then she stepped into the car, the driver closed the door, and the limo disappeared into the night.

The weary young man walked back home, sat down in a chair beside Bethanie, kissed her on the cheek, and then covered her with a blanket.

As he turned off the light switch and started to shut the door, Liam looked back and quietly said, "Goodnight, Sweet Mother. . . ."

CHAPTER 19

The day finally came for Liam to leave with the team, and he was once again up early. He finished packing, showered, and although he was too nervous to eat, Liam walked to the main house to get some fruit and snacks to take with him.

To his surprise, Bethanie was already there. Alberto had already stopped in to check on her and she was up early, so he guided her on a light walk over to the main house to wait on Liam. The two were now sitting in chairs near the window, and Alberto motioned to Liam to join them.

"Your driver is waiting whenever you're ready. Anything else we can help with? Are you having breakfast today?"

Liam shook his head and shrugged. "I don't think so—and no, I don't have an appetite right now." The young man then put his arms around Alberto and his mom. "Thank you for everything. I love you both."

Bethanie beamed. "Give it your all—we will be cheering for you, Son. I am proud of you."

The young man smiled, headed to the kitchen to grab his snacks, then walked out the door to begin the first leg of his journey with destiny. . . .

When they arrived in San Juan, the team took a short bus ride to their hotel, got checked in quickly, and headed to the stadium for a morning workout. Apparently, several other Caribbean teams had the same idea, and a mixture of different languages could be heard echoing through the stadium on the humid Puerto Rican morning.

Each athlete from the Dominican Republic knew the role they would play. They went to the center of the field, did some stretching and team chanting, then split off to practice their specialties. The meet would start tomorrow morning, so this was a great opportunity for athletes to squeeze in one more practice and hear some much-appreciated pep talks.

After about an hour, Coach José pulled the team together and ended the session. He complimented each athlete and then finished by saying, "Let's head back to the hotel and grab a bite to eat. We can take it easy the rest of the day."

The players nodded their approval, and as they filed out of the stadium, the young athletes stared in awe at the magnificent surroundings, and noted the other teams who were wrapping up their own practices: Anguilla, St. Barts, St. Kitts, Barbados, the Bahamas . . . it seemed all the Caribbean was united in one stadium.

As they marched toward the exit, Liam looked back one more time to take in the scene, excited nerves running up his spine.

After a light lunch at the hotel, a local guide led the team on a walking tour around the old city of San Juan. There was so much beauty and cultural diversity to enjoy, including authentic restaurants lining the streets. Liam's jaw dropped as their tour guide pointed out the bronze statues of the mighty conquistadors from years past like Juan Ponce de León and Christopher Columbus. He thought about the struggles they had faced, which only served to strengthen the young man's resolve.

As the day wound down, the athletes gathered for dinner in a private room at the hotel restaurant. Once everyone had finished their meal, Coach José asked for quiet, holding his hands high.

"Okay, everyone, it's been a great day, and tomorrow is what we have been working toward."

The team clapped and cheered, then grew silent again as the coach continued.

"But let's remember, this is simply about giving the sport all we have. It's about knowing that when we finish each event, we can walk off the track or field, and be sure there is nothing else we could have done to succeed."

The teammates smiled, then José stood and put his hand out. The team slowly stood and reached their own hands toward the center. When all athletes were represented, they looked to Liam, who cried out, "Go, Dominican Republic!" Everyone joined in a synchronized echo of Liam's words that seemed to ring across the city.

The next morning after breakfast, as the squad made their way to the stadium, they saw the stands bursting with spectators!

One of the athletes turned to Liam and whispered, "I don't care how many times I go to these regional and national meets, it never ceases to amaze me that so many people come out to see us do what we do. It's . . . humbling."

When the competitors entered the stadium, a booming voice blared over the public address system, "Now entering the stadium . . . the Dominican Republic national team!"

The coach and athletes waved to the crowd, and the spectators showed their appreciation by screaming even louder. As they walked in and claimed their designated area, the cheers died down, and the Dominicans began to take off their warm-up jackets and start to stretch in preparation.

Right then, however, the stadium erupted again in cheers. It seemed to Liam to be twice as loud as when his team had entered. Confused, he looked at his teammates.

Emmanuel, the high jumper, looked at Liam and rolled his eyes. "The Jamaicans are always the favorites—can't you tell?" He chuckled.

Another Dominican athlete turned to Liam. "And THERE is the main reason."

Liam followed the athlete's point and saw a lean, tall, dark-skinned man of about twenty, waving broadly to the crowd and flashing a bright smile. Liam recognized the man immediately. "That's Alton Williams, the hundred-meter-dash legend! Everyone says he will win the world championship this year."

Emmanuel nodded. "Yep, that's what they say." Then he added with a grin, "But they haven't seen Liam Pérez yet."

Liam cocked a curious eyebrow and smiled. "Yeah, maybe you're right."

At that moment, the All-Caribbean meet was declared to be officially open as the crowd roared its approval. As the events took place, Liam watched the athletes' feats in amazement. Throughout the day, each country claimed wins, runners-up . . . or sometimes nothing at all.

Liam began to break out in a sweat as he began focusing on his race.

With only a few events left, the Dominican Republic surprisingly found themselves in the lead. It was a dream come true for Coach José who had never led a team so close to a victory at this meet.

As the triple jump closed out, the team moved ahead on the leaderboard with another first place. The pole vault win went to Jamaica, and with another win in the high jump, Jamaica was just behind the Dominican Republic.

Coach José squinted into the bright Puerto Rican sun at the scoreboard, and much to his chagrin, Grenada was gaining ground also—now close behind, in third place. He nervously raked his hand through his dark hair.

At that moment, it occurred to Liam that if he could capture first place in his event, it would put the team unbeatably ahead going into the final event, the four-hundred-meter relay.

Finally, the one-hundred-meter dash was announced over the intercom, and as the athletes lined up in their lanes, Liam found himself next to Jamaica's Alton Williams. He could feel himself trembling uncontrollably in the steamy Puerto Rican stadium.

Liam . . . you were made for this, he assured himself.

Deafening cheers arose from the crowd as the runners took their positions, and Liam felt as if he were sandwiched between the track-and-field version of the conquistadors he had seen yesterday. *Everyone* in every lane was great.

Liam stood nervously, hoping the spectators could not see his shaking arms and legs. Alton Williams, the sinewy Jamaican, turned and looked blankly at the Dominican runner, and next he scanned the lanes to see his other competitors. Then, as if none of it mattered to him, Alton simply turned gracefully away and stared straight ahead, like in a deep trance.

At that moment, Bethanie Pérez, who had been fixated on the television all day, moved to the edge of her seat at home in Santa Guaro, anxiously wringing her hands. Maria stood beside her, as did Alberto, trying to keep the woman calm.

"Bethanie, you must relax. This stress can't be good for you." His upturned palms matched the pleading in his voice—but that urging seemed to go unheeded by Bethanie.

"Alberto, I am trying, but I can't help it. This is so important to him . . . "

Right then, Liam Pérez heard those words he had come to know so very well: "On your marks . . . set . . ." The starting pistol fired, and the runners left in a blaze. The Dominican sprinter immediately fell behind, and his mother involuntarily sprang to her feet. "Go, Liam, go!"

As if he had heard her, Liam's eyes widened while he desperately picked up speed to match that of the charging Jamaican. Then, out of the corner of the Dominican runner's eye, he saw Michael Clarke, the slim, muscular runner from Barbados, getting closer to them both.

No, no, no! he thought to himself.

The distance ticked off quickly. The crowd screamed wildly. The three runners were now perfectly even, sweat glistening on each of them, and then . . .

It was over.

Alton Williams raised his arms in victory, and his teammates poured onto the track and lifted the Jamaican over their heads.

In what seemed like seconds, the official scoreboard flashed the race results:

Williams/Jamaica

Pérez/Dominican Republic

Clarke/Barbados

Liam felt as if he would be sick. He continued to walk around the track, shaking and trying to catch his breath, when someone came up behind him and put their strong arms around him.

"Coach José!" Liam felt the tears well up in his eyes. "I'm so . . . sorry," the boy stuttered.

A broad smile crossed José's face as he eased off his embrace, spun his team member around and replied, "Well, you should be. I mean, you let probably the best hundred-meter runner in the world beat you by a hundredth of a second . . . in your first major race. How could you?"

He laughed, placed his hands on the young man's shoulders and looked into his moistening eyes. "I could not be prouder of you, Liam Pérez."

Liam's tears poured out now as he hugged his coach in front of the cheering stadium and the press snapped pictures.

"Liam, do you know who those cheers are for?"

The weary runner looked around, and then shook his head. "I suppose they are for Alton."

José gestured across the stadium, then replied slowly, "No, that happened a while ago—you've lost track of time. Those cheers are for *you*."

The young man's forehead creased in confusion. "But, I didn't win, Coach."

"Liam, these people know what you did today was bordering on the miraculous. They have heard of your skill and your heart. They also know there will be many days ahead for you, and they were here to see the beginning of that greatness. Wave to the crowd, Liam the Great."

With that, Liam turned and waved to all corners of the erupting stadium. At that moment, the entire Dominican team poured onto the track and swarmed around the young man. Seeing the camaraderie, the crowd now raised their level of cheering . . . for the entire Dominican Republic team.

Back in Santa Guaro, Liam's mother's heart was full as she, Alberto, and Maria watched everything unfold. She saw the crowd cheer for her son, and she was elated. But she also knew Liam's feelings too well—and she knew the sadness that must be crushing him.

Staring at the television, Bethanie gently placed her hand across her heart.

As tears rolled down her soft cheeks, she smiled and said shakily, "I am proud of you, my boy. . . ."

CHAPTER 20

The team ended up finishing the meet in an impressive second place, with Jamaica solidly ahead after a final win in the four-hundred-meter relay.

Loading up the bus for the trip back to the airport, the Dominican competitors were surrounded by fans and autograph seekers. The attention was a much-appreciated consolation as the team began the bittersweet trip home. There was much to be grateful for, yet the athletes also realized they had been in striking distance of a major championship.

On the flight home, Liam talked to his teammates about the competition, and he was relieved that they harbored nothing but good feelings toward him.

"I was so afraid I had let everyone down," he confided to José.

The coach hesitated and then turned back to Liam. "Remember what we say: 'As long as we give everything we have, there is no way we could let anyone down.' It was clear that you did that very thing, Liam."

"Thank you, Coach," the young man said with a toothy grin. "Next stop, The World Games?"

The coach gave Liam a high five. "I think that's a perfect next stop." Then he added with a wink, "Who knows, you may just run into your Jamaican friend again . . ."

Alberto was waiting when the team bus pulled into Santa Guaro from the airport. He stepped out of his limousine and clapped for the team loudly. Recognizing Alberto as one of the most successful businesspeople in the Dominican Republic, the athletes waved and smiled broadly.

"Thank you so much, Mr. Rodriguez!" they shouted back.

José stepped off the bus toward Alberto. "Thank you, my friend. I am so proud of the team . . . and of Liam."

Alberto nodded and shook the leader's outstretched hand. "It was clearly a team effort—and they had some expert coaching." He grinned.

Liam made his way off the bus, and his eyes locked in on Alberto. With a fervent wave, the young man ran over and threw his arms around him. Before Liam could speak, Alberto leaned away and lifted the boy's chin. "I am so proud of you—and so is your Momma."

Liam's face brightened. "How is she doing?"

Alberto shrugged and grinned. "Well, she's a lot better, but it's a wonder she didn't get whiplash from jumping up and down and yelling at the TV during your track meet."

They threw back their heads and laughed at the thought of Bethanie pouring herself into the televised event, screaming for her son.

But Liam said in a small voice, "I . . . hope I didn't let either of you down. I tried my best, and . . ."

Alberto held up a finger to his own lips. "There will be none of that, young man. We could not be any prouder of you—and the whole country feels the same way."

Liam cocked his head as Alberto continued.

"Liam, you have given this country hope. Seeing a young man compete like you did, with such courage and determination, and at such a young age—it was incredibly inspiring. The whole team did a beautiful job."

Liam managed a slight smile. "Can we go home now, Alberto? I want to see my mom, and I'm so tired."

"Of course," he replied. The two men stepped into the limousine as the driver lifted Liam's bag and put it into the trunk. Then they were off, making their way back to Alberto's farm.

There was a great deal of chatter in the car on the way home, even from the driver, who glanced at Liam in the rearview mirror to ask, "Were you nervous?"

Liam shook his head. "Not really."

When the driver shot a questioning glance at the young man, Liam laughed and added, "More like . . . scared to death."

Everyone chuckled, and the driver crossed his hand over his heart. "I would have been terrified, but you looked so calm."

Liam expressed his gratitude, and a few minutes later, the limo pulled into the compound, passed through the gate, and pulled up to the main house.

The young athlete looked out the window and breathed, "Home sweet home," to which Alberto responded with wide grin.

Liam hopped out of the car, and the driver gestured for the boy to go inside. "I will get your bags—go see your mom."

When Liam flung the door open, there was Bethanie, standing in the den, waiting with open arms for her son. "I am so happy to see you, Son."

The boy reached out, put his arms tenderly around his mother, and then pulled back slowly. "How are you, Momma? Your bandage is gone—that must be a good thing."

She shook her head. "Yes, I got rid of that old thing—and I am doing much better." Hesitating, she added, "Now, let's talk about my superhero son."

Liam laughed and hugged his mother tighter. "Ah, Momma. It was great. It was such an incredible experience and . . . I was *so* close!"

His mother smiled and then wagged a playful finger at him. "There will be plenty of other times."

Right then, the kitchen door opened, and Liam's eyes welled up as he saw the beautiful young woman enter, carrying a cake.

"Maria!"

He ran over, and before he could put his arms around her, she glanced down at the culinary delight.

"Don't squish your cake, Liam the Great!"

The young man's gaze fell to the letters on the cake which read, "WE ARE PROUD OF YOU!"

Liam smiled as she put down the cake and then wrapped her arms around him. "Congratulations, Liam! The whole country is proud of you, too."

Alberto joined them, and Eliza followed with plates and forks. She placed them delicately on the kitchen table before expertly slicing up the cake. Savoring it together, the group sat and caught up with Liam on his last few days.

After the celebration, Liam politely excused himself as his eyes became heavy. "Thank you all for everything. I can't wait to share more with each of you, but I've got to go rest . . . I never knew competing against Jamaicans could be so exhausting!"

He laughed, walked around, and hugged each person at the table before heading to his bedroom at home, where he lay down on his bed . . . and fell sound asleep.

After two days off, it was back to practice for the entire team. Although their first workout was light, it was a good chance for the team to get together again and celebrate all the good things that had happened in San Juan.

Toward the end of the practice, Coach José spoke. "Okay everyone, as fantastic as it was, that meet is behind us. We have less than ten months to prepare for an even bigger event—the World Games in Saint Lucia."

There was complete silence in the group as José continued, "As you know, the All-Caribbean meet qualified our entire team to compete in the World Games, but I must tell you—the stakes will be higher than they were in Puerto Rico."

The athletes exchanged wide-eyed looks, and José added, "Listen, this was a perfect warm-up and a test to see if you have what it takes. Now we know you all have *exactly* what it takes. Saint Lucia will be new for all of us. We have never had athletes that were good enough to qualify, and the fact that each of you qualified tells me we are ready."

The coach reached out his hand, and one by one, they placed their hands on top of each other's. Liam slowly placed his hand on top and cried, "Go, Dominican Republic!" in a way that once again motivated the entire group to chant the same.

CHAPTER 21

Time moved quickly over the next ten months.

With every practice, Liam and his teammates got better and better. They attended more meets across the Caribbean and South America, and the Dominican squad dominated nearly every one of them. The Jamaicans, however, seemed to be avoiding the meets in which the Dominican Republic team was entered.

José addressed the group's suspicions. "It is likely part of their competitive strategy," he would answer. "We know that the Jamaicans are not keen on competing with us unless they have to—we were so close to beating them last time."

The young athletes stared into their wise coach's eyes as he continued with his theory. "I think they want to save up their courage for when they know they will *have* to compete with us again—in Saint Lucia."

Liam, now more mature and comfortable in speaking up, piped in, "They can run . . . but they can't hide!" The athletes loved those words, and it became a mantra during their meets and practices.

Liam was increasing in skill—and in popularity, although his humility never wavered. Even at school, he was just "Liam" to his classmates. Quite often, when a reporter would stop by the school to gain an interview and picture of him, Liam would grab one of his classmates and pull them into the photo with a wide grin.

Maria continued to get closer to Liam and his whole family. It was not unusual for her to spend weekends with the Pérezes and Alberto at the farm and be available to help any way she could. For Bethanie, Maria was the daughter she never had. They all took trips across the Dominican Republic and attended openings of new chocolate factories together. Maria had undoubtedly become part of the family.

Alberto and Bethanie's bond also grew stronger, as they came to believe they had been put into each other's lives for a reason—and Liam was thrilled.

Then one evening, when the family was having dinner, the phone rang, which Bethanie answered. She turned to Liam. "It's for you, Son—someone from the United States."

Liam crinkled up his nose. "Who is it?"

She shook her head. "He says he's a sports agent."

"Why is he calling *me*?"

Bethanie laughed and covered the phone. "Maybe if you take his call, he'll tell you."

Maria giggled.

Liam said little, except for the occasional grunt and one "uh-huh." After a few moments, he told the man goodbye and hung up.

The table was quiet as Liam sat back down.

Bethanie broke the silence and turned her palms up in curiosity. "Well?"

The young man took a deep breath and responded, "He said his name was Tyler Dickens, and he's from a sports management agency in Los Angeles—the McDowell Group."

The family exchanged glances as Liam continued. "He wants to come watch me compete at the World Games. If things go like he thinks they will, he would like to represent me."

Liam paused and looked at his mother. "The firm handles the biggest athletes in the world, Momma. He wanted to find out if I was interested in talking with them, and if so, he said he would reach out to you and Alberto to explain how their company works."

Bethanie ran her fingers through her hair and glanced at Alberto.

"It sounds legitimate," Alberto offered. "I have friends who are professional athletes, and they work with agents—the McDowell Group is very well respected. I can have someone check out this specific agent to make sure he's really with McDowell."

Liam continued, "Tyler told me their firm isn't usually interested in runners, but someone insisted he should consider me because they had met me before and were impressed. He happened to be in San Juan during the All-Caribbean meet, and he turned on the TV right as I was starting the race with Alton Williams. He said he's been following me ever since." Liam paused and looked at his mother who now had tears in her eyes.

"Liam the Great," she said softly.

Liam shrugged. "Well, we'll see how it plays out. Who knows if I'll hear anything back from him."

Wanting to change the subject, Liam turned to Maria and offered, "So, what do you think about coming to Saint Lucia next month with us?"

Bethanie broke into a wide grin and added, "I talked about it with your parents, Maria, and they both gave their okay—if you would like to go."

"Really?" Maria clapped loudly, and reached over and hugged her boyfriend. But then, just as quickly, her mood became crestfallen. "I . . . my family . . . could never afford that. I mean . . ."

Alberto interrupted the girl and waved a dismissive hand. "That will be taken care of. Don't give it a second thought."

She gazed wide-eyed at Alberto and turned to Bethanie, then jumped out of her chair and hugged each of them, one after another. "Thank you, yes! I would *love* to go!"

It was now a week before the World Games, and Liam's times were faster than they had ever been. Coach José worked additional hours with the eager young athlete every week, and Liam was up early each morning putting in even more hours.

One afternoon, at the end of a team workout, José pulled Liam aside and pointed to a casually-dressed gentleman who appeared to be in his early twenties, standing at the fence. "Liam, that's Roberto Cortez from the Dominican news. He wants to speak with you."

Liam finished his last bit of stretching and then stood.

"Hi, Mr. Cortez," the young man offered politely.

The reporter extended his hand. "Please, call me Roberto. It's great to meet you, Liam. I wanted to ask you a few questions, if I could."

Liam shook his hand and shrugged. "Sure."

The young reporter pulled out his pad and scanned the scribbled notes. "Liam, I understand you were on the boat that capsized years ago near Antigua."

Liam hesitated, then palmed the back of his neck. "I don't have people ask me much about that anymore— thankfully. I'd rather you not write about that."

The man closed his pad and nodded. "Okay, I won't. I don't like to talk about it either."

The runner tilted his head in confusion, so Roberto explained, "I was on that boat, too."

Liam's jaw dropped.

"I was just a little older than you were. Everything was so chaotic that night, you might not remember what I'm about to tell you."

Liam nodded tentatively as the young man continued.

"My mom was pregnant at the time with my little brother, and she couldn't move quickly. When the ship started sinking, people were pushing us out of the way, and then she fell, and we were both almost trampled. I tried to help her up—but I couldn't do it alone."

The reporter paused as he relived the horrible moment, fighting back tears. "You were running past us and saw it happen. Even as young as you were, you and Mr. Rodriguez stopped and helped us. After that, someone else found us a lifeboat, and ours was one of the last to get off before the ship sank. I've always thought it was a miracle—if it hadn't been for you and Mr. Rodriguez, we surely would have died."

Liam reached out and embraced the man as the memory started to return. "Yes, yes, I do remember that now!" He shook his head in sympathy. "I'm so sorry . . . how is your mother doing?"

A smile appeared on the man's face. "Doing very well, thank you. After she and my dad split up, she remarried, and now she lives with my stepfather and my little brother in Quito."

"That's wonderful. Please tell her I said hi." Then Liam paused and added, "Again, I would rather not have anything written about the ship incident. I have tried to put that in the past, quite often unsuccessfully, I'm sad to say. I am grateful I was able to help your family, but the memories have tormented me for years . . . even though I know that event helped make me who I am."

The young reporter nodded and held up his hand. "I totally understand. Consider it sealed. But now, could we talk about the World Games?"

Liam nodded again, brightening. "Of course. Now, between the meet and my team, you'll have a hard time getting me to quit talking!" Liam threw back his head and laughed.

The reporter proceeded to speak cordially with the young man, asking him all sorts of questions about how they were preparing for the meet, how they were feeling about the competition, and anything else he could think of about The Games. After a few minutes, the young men shook hands and agreed to get together after the competition ended.

Liam then jogged over to meet up with his teammates and Coach José to officially conclude practice.

"Okay, team, we are getting close to the big event. Everyone ready?"

The teammates all smiled, and José added, "Let's finish these practices strong—and then take that title home!" The group cheered their approval, and the coach grinned and walked off the track as the team followed.

The grueling practices continued daily until it was almost time for the World Games. The day before the team was scheduled to fly out, Liam's classmates had decorated the school in honor of their friend, who was now competing in one of the biggest track and field events in the world. It was a total surprise for Liam when he entered the building, and after celebrating, they all posed for a group picture with their pal, chanting "Go get 'em, Liam!" The young runner profusely thanked the group, then headed for home—with Maria by his side.

"I'm so excited to be going with you and your family, Liam. I promise I won't be any trouble or get in the way." She grinned and poked him playfully.

"Yes, you have always been a lot of trouble." He laughed and then poignantly added, "Maria, I really am so happy you're going to be there. I have to tell you . . . I'm scared."

She cocked her head in surprise. "Scared? You? I'm surprised, Liam—I didn't think anything scared you."

Liam cracked a smile and said, "I just don't want to let people down. I don't want to let the country down, or my mom and Alberto, or Coach . . . or you."

Maria stopped walking, pivoted toward the young man, and reached over to gently hold his hands. "Mr. Pérez," she started in a silly way, "first of all, you can never let me down. I am already so proud of you, I don't know how I could be any prouder. I think the same could be said for your mom and Alberto, and Coach José . . . and as far as the country, well, the Dominican Republic is lucky to have you."

Liam squeezed her hands, leaned over, and kissed her lightly on the cheek. "You always know what to say, you know that?"

She grinned. "It's all true, Liam. Plus, remember what Coach José says . . . 'Give it everything you've got, and there is nothing else anyone can ask for.'"

Liam palmed the back of his neck and then smiled. "I guess you're right—then again, you're always right."

Maria tossed her hair and laughed. "Remember that when we get married!"

Liam shook his head and rolled his eyes in jest. "I guess I set myself up for that one."

The pair made their way back to the cocoa ranch, chatting the whole time about what St. Lucia would be like. The conversation was refreshingly full of laughter and lightheartedness—something Liam realized would be foreign to him when he stepped onto the track in two days . . .

CHAPTER 22

The team arrived right on time at the airport, and when they boarded their plane, the excitement was palpable. On the flight, passengers would approach the athletes to ask for pictures to be taken with them and their families, which the young, emerging sports celebrities all were happy to do.

Once the plane landed in Saint Lucia, the media swamped them, asking the team and their coach who would win the championship.

Then a reporter shoved his microphone in front of Liam and asked pointedly, "So, what do you expect from Alton Williams this time, Liam? Are you ready for him?"

The young man paused, then replied calmly, "I wish him the best. My job is to run as fast as I can, and to represent the Dominican Republic as well as I can. Beyond that, I have no control over the outcome or what other runners do."

The reporter raised an eyebrow at the composed response, and then—doubtless hoping for a juicier comment—moved on to another athlete.

When the team finally arrived at the hotel in St. Lucia, they took a few minutes to unpack before meeting for lunch downstairs. Bethanie, Maria, and Alberto joined the group, and listened happily to all the excited chatter as the team talked about the World Games.

After lunch, the Dominicans headed over to the stadium. They had practiced their skills hundreds of times by now, but today, they wanted to go through everything once more—just to be sure.

Liam ran a solid time, but did not want to push himself too much. As he finished, he turned to his left and spotted Alton Williams. The cocky Jamaican flashed a toothy grin at the young man from the Dominican Republic.

"Better run faster than that, my friend!" he jeered.

Liam shook his head and laughed, then turned and walked away, unperturbed.

After another half hour of practice, the coach pulled his squad together. "Okay, team, let's head back to the hotel. We'll relax a little bit by the pool and then turn in early after dinner."

He smiled, scanned the group, and added, "Big day tomorrow, everyone."

The young athletes raised their hands jubilantly and cheered. Then the group gathered their belongings, jumped into the waiting van, and took the short trip back to their hotel for the evening.

The night passed quickly, and the next morning, all the Dominican contestants were up early. They met for breakfast and piled back into the van for the short trip back over to the stadium.

Like in Puerto Rico, the atmosphere was electric. There were fans everywhere. The massive stadium, which was also used for cricket championships, was filling up fast. As the Dominican squad passed through security and entered the arena, cheers reverberated all through the stands.

Waving excitedly at the spectators, the team headed over to their designated area to begin their warm-up exercises. At one point, José glanced up at the massive turnout of fans, then looked back at his athletes and evenly offered, "I think these folks are going to witness history being made today." He smiled and pulled the team together to await the opening gunshot, signifying the start of the competition.

Once it was fired, the athletes hastily took their places. The events went by quickly, and the Dominican Republic was off to a great start—tied for the lead with Jamaica, as many had predicted.

The crowd roared with fervor as the action became more and more intense. The different countries were all fielding their best athletic representatives, and the supporters' excitement was worthy of such a world-class event.

The intense heat, however, was less welcome. The St. Lucia summer sun and humidity combined made it feel like one hundred and ten degrees.

As the championship neared its end, the crowd was ecstatic to see that the Dominican Republic was in first place, just ahead of the Jamaican team. With the other countries out of contention for the top two spots—it appeared to be a perfect rematch between the All-Caribbean meet finalists. Like in Puerto Rico, if Liam could somehow earn first place in the one-hundred-meter dash, it would ensure a World Games victory for the Dominican team over the Jamaicans. If not, then the final event, the four-hundred-meter dash, would be the deciding race.

There were plenty of other athletes from all over the world, but now, all eyes were on the two Caribbean runners—Liam and Alton.

As all the sprinters took their places, the two superstars again found themselves in lanes next to each other. A hush swept over the stadium as the men waited for the starting gun. Alton turned his glare to his various opponents before settling on Liam. The Jamaican sneered, which the young Dominican calmly ignored.

In the stands, Alberto, Maria, and Bethanie sat nervously. The three locked arms together, waiting . . .

"On your marks . . . set . . ."

The starting shot rang out, and all the runners took off at a blistering pace. The noise of the crowd was deafening, but Liam did not notice it as he surged ahead. Alton seemed to effortlessly move up right beside him, the runners' arms firing like pistons. The Jamaican runner inched ahead . . . then moved even farther ahead.

In the stands, Bethanie screamed her encouragement over the crowd as she gripped Alberto's arm anxiously.

Right then, Liam pulled even with Alton, as the other runners gradually faded behind them into the pack. Alton inched forward, and then Liam recovered. Suddenly, Liam seemed to pull from a superhuman reservoir of energy as he pushed past the Jamaican. Meters from the finish line, the young Dominican stretched his head forward as far as he possibly could . . . right in time.

Liam Pérez . . . was a world champion.

The crowd erupted in jubilant cheers as Liam and the other runners continued jogging slowly around the track. Then another massive wave of cheering caused the young Dominican runner to look up and see "World Record—Liam Pérez, Dominican Republic" on the scoreboard.

The team piled out onto the track and lifted Liam over their heads. He laughed with exhaustion, surprise, relief, and joy. . . . Then, out of the corner of his eye, he saw a young, dark-haired woman running toward him, pushing through the crowd.

"Maria!" Liam sprinted to her, catching his breath as he ran. Finally reaching through the crowd, he pulled her close and held on as the spectators patted him on the back and congratulated the other athletes as well.

With wide eyes, he yelled above the crowd, "Maria, I can't believe it—we did it!"

She smiled broadly, then wrapped her arms around tightly around him. "Yes, my gentle warrior, yes. . . ."

Once the madness had settled, the team gathered for the trophy presentation.

"Third place," the announcer began, "goes to Germany." The crowd applauded.

"Second place goes to . . . Jamaica." Again, a unified cheer arose.

"First place in the World Games—for the first time in history—goes to . . . the Dominican Republic!"

The applause was thunderous as the team raised their hands and their voices in unbridled celebration. Coach José accepted the winning trophy and held it high over his head, smiling from ear to ear.

No one cheered louder than Bethanie and Alberto. In the bleachers, they pointed and waved happily to

Liam, who caught their eyes and waved back as he stood with his arm around Maria.

The cheering seemed to go on for hours, and when it finally died down, the team was immediately pulled in all directions by a host of reporters from around the world.

After they had all been interviewed for quotes, the coach motioned for his athletes to head back to the locker room. On their way, they waved to the fans one last time.

Once they made it to the locker room, the team broke into a jubilant chant. "Dominican, Dominican, Dominican!"

Coach José walked around and congratulated the athletes one by one. When he reached Liam, he whispered, "There is someone outside who would like to speak with you."

Liam cocked a curious eyebrow, wondering why this wouldn't wait, but José smiled and gestured toward the door. "Just say hello to them and come back—you'll have plenty of time to talk later."

Liam, still unsure of the visitor, walked out and was greeted by a middle-aged, fit gentleman wearing a pin-striped suit.

"Hi, Liam. I'm Tyler Dickens."

Liam immediately recalled the American sports agent's name from the phone call back home. He extended a hand, which the agent shook heartily.

"I take it you remember me—and our phone discussion?"

Liam ran his fingers nervously through his thick black hair, and smiled. "Well, I have to say, it's not every day that athletes in the Dominican Republic get a call from an agent. I kind of thought you had pranked me." He grinned.

The agent threw back his head and laughed. "I can assure you I wasn't 'pranking' you." He reached into his pocket and pulled out an envelope. "This is an offer from my company—The McDowell Group—for ten million dollars to represent you."

Liam felt the blood drain from his face. "Wait. What? Ten million US dollars?"

The man shrugged. "That's just the start. You will have other sources of income too, including endorsements and bonuses. We will help you with all that."

"I, um, don't really know what to say," Liam stuttered. "I'd like to talk it over with my mom first."

The man patted Liam on the shoulder. "Of course. Just let me know as soon as you can, Liam." With that, Tyler Dickens turned to walk away, but he pivoted and looked back at the young Dominican.

"Liam, it's not just what you have done—and what you continue to do—in your sport . . . it's who you are that appeals to us. As I mentioned to you on the phone, a friend of mine told me I should consider signing you.

He was exceptionally impressed when he met you, and I agree with him . . . you are a special person and will be a great representative."

Liam cocked his head in curiosity. "May I ask who that was?"

The agent paused. "Roberto Cortez—a reporter friend of mine. He said he met you when he was very young, something about being on a cruise—he didn't really go into too much detail." He smiled.

A wide grin appeared on the young man's face. "Yes, sir . . . I do remember him."

With that, the agent nodded and added kindly, "We look forward to hearing from you, Liam," then he turned and faded down the hallway.

Liam, his mind still reeling, walked back into the locker room where the athletes were celebrating.

Coach José smiled at him knowingly. "You alright, Liam?"

"I'm not sure, Coach . . . but I think I will be."

The coach laughed as the celebration raged on. Soon after, Liam dismissed himself to connect with his family. He found them standing on the field, surrounded by reporters. Not wanting to draw attention, Liam waited for an opportune moment to grab his mother gently by the arm. Catching on, Maria and Alberto followed.

"Momma, you're not going to believe it . . ."

When Liam relayed the news to the three, a cheer went up as the group hugged and laughed. Alberto smiled. "I double-checked with my sources. Tyler and The McDowell Group work with top athletes all over the world. What do you say, Liam?"

Liam turned to his mother. "I want to do this, Momma."

Bethanie put her arms around her son and said softly, "Liam, your time has come. Your talents and story will be an inspiration to the world, and this offer will help you reach even more people. Yes, I agree—you should accept." He nodded.

Maria glanced at the young man as he then turned and looked into her eyes. He reached into the pocket of his team jacket. "I almost forgot—I got you a little something, and I have been waiting for the right time to give it to you."

With that, Liam dropped to one knee and opened the box. "Maria, will you . . . make me the happiest man in the world, and marry me?"

She covered her mouth, and her eyes became like saucers, but she was speechless.

Liam raised an eyebrow and then offered jokingly to his mother, "Wow, I think she likes it even more than the one I gave her in middle school!"

Maria burst out laughing and pulled the young man up and into her arms. "I cannot think of anything I would rather do, Liam Pérez. Yes, I will! Yes! Yes!"

She turned to Bethanie and Alberto, then smiled and pointed a playful finger. "You knew about this the whole time, didn't you?"

Bethanie grinned. "Of course not." Then she shrugged and added, "Not until a few days ago anyway." The three laughed, and all pulled together and embraced.

Alberto squeezed the shoulders of the young couple and said with a broad smile, "I see . . . some great days ahead."

CHAPTER 23

The next day, the flight back to the Dominican Republic was a jubilant one. The pilot even announced the presence of "the new world champions" on the flight. The passengers applauded wildly, and the athletes raised their hands and waved to the admirers.

When the flight landed, there were throngs of fans waiting. The young track stars hadn't experienced this kind of fame, and they relished the adoration. When they were all off the flight and standing in the Santo Domingo terminal together, Coach José shared with the crowd how proud he was of his team and the effort they had put into their training.

"The unusual thing about this group is that there is not one selfish person on the entire team. Anyone in this squad would happily sacrifice for any other teammate. These are not just great track-and-field champions, they are also champion people."

The fans broke out into applause, and the team thanked everyone for coming out as they headed toward the awaiting bus that would carry them back to their meeting point at the school.

When they finally arrived, the team said their goodbyes as each athlete split off and started toward their waiting rides to take them back to their homes.

"Take a few days off, champs," José called to them. "You earned it!" he said with a grin.

Only Liam, Alberto, Maria, and Bethanie were left with Coach José, whose fatigue was finally starting to show.

Bethanie reached out to him. "None of this would have been possible without you, José. We are so grateful for everything you've done. Thank you from the bottom of my heart." She embraced José, and his lips turned upward in appreciation.

"To work with this team is a gift." Then he added, "And to work with Liam is a gift among gifts. Truly, I am the one who is grateful." He crossed his hand over his heart, and the three of them reciprocated.

Alberto's limousine pulled up. The four of them waved goodbye to the coach, then they entered the vehicle, as the smiling driver welcomed them home to the Dominican Republic.

The ride back was short, gratefully, but once the group arrived at the farm, they were ready for a quick bite of dinner and then an early night.

After they unloaded their luggage and washed up, they connected back at the kitchen table of the main house, as usual.

Once his guests were seated, Alberto stood and looked around at the group of happy yet exhausted friends and family members.

"We have so much to be grateful for tonight," he began. "In addition to Liam and Maria's engagement, the World Games win, and the forthcoming signing of Liam's contract, I would like to add one more thing . . ."

The others raised their eyebrows and exchanged puzzled glances.

Alberto turned to Bethanie, dropped to one knee, and said with a gentle smile, "We can't be left out of the fun, Bethanie . . . will you marry me?"

He opened a small box that was sitting inconspicuously off to the side of the table, as Bethanie's eyes grew wide. Seeing the beautiful ring, she threw her arms around the excited man and enthusiastically replied, "In the words of Maria . . . Yes! Yes! Yes!"

Liam turned to his new fiancée and added with a broad grin, "And in the words of Alberto, I think this family is going to have some great days ahead. . . ."

Find more inspirational adventures at
www.skipjohnsonauthor.com

MAY I ASK A FAVOR?

Thank you for reading my book! Would you do me a favor and take a moment to write a short review on Amazon? Reviews are extremely important to authors like me, and if you would share your thoughts so others can find out about my writing, I would be truly grateful.

If you leave a review, feel free to let me know by dropping me an email at skipjohnsonauthor1@gmail.com so I can personally thank you.

WANT TO GET WEEKLY INSPIRATION FROM ME?

To get new, weekly inspirational stories and articles at no charge—and to stay updated on my release dates for new books—send an email request to me at skipjohnsonauthor1@gmail.com. I'll also send you an inspirational e-book of mine as a thank-you!

ABOUT SKIP JOHNSON

Skip Johnson is an award-winning inspirational author whose goal is to empower, inspire, and enrich the lives of his readers.

He is known for his easygoing style of adventurous storytelling, with rich elements of spirituality, mysticism, and personal growth woven throughout his books. One prominent aspect of Skip's writing is how he takes readers on symbolic journeys of self-discovery and enlightenment. His characters often find themselves on treks to faraway places where meetings with wise, mystical mentors lead readers to contemplate their own personal and spiritual journeys and how their lives can be more fulfilling and joyful.

His storytelling is simple yet profound, allowing readers from all walks of life to extract and quickly apply the nuggets of wisdom, compassion, and peacefulness that permeate the pages of his narratives. He uses crystal-clear imagery to create the feeling for readers of being right beside each character on their life-changing, heroic journey in every saga.

Skip's books are both spiritual and practical. Each story encourages readers to look inside themselves for the magic, courage, and strength that is often deeply hidden within themselves, patiently waiting to be released to powerfully impact the world.

Based in Georgia, Skip himself has traveled many paths, including that of a motivational speaker, a business leader, a master tennis professional, and a world traveler. These experiences have shaped his writing, and the wisdom and insights woven into each story leave readers filled with wonder, gratitude, and enthusiasm for the days ahead.

In addition to *The Gentle Warrior*, Skip is the author of the novels *The Mystic's Gift*, *The Gentleman's Journey*, *The Treasure in Antigua*, *The Lottery Winner's Greatest Ride*, *The Statue's Secret*, *The Cobbler of Cape Town*, and *The Innkeeper's Journal*, as well as the nonfiction books *Grateful for Everything*, *Hidden Jewels of Happiness*, and *Starting Each Day in a Powerful Way*. His works have earned The Maxy Awards Book of the Year, the International Book Award, and the Nautilus Silver Award. They have also been finalists in The Eric Hoffer Book Awards, The Feathered Quill Book Awards, and The Wishing Shelf Book Awards (UK).